Curses And Wonders

Mary Catelli

Published by Wizard's Wood Press, 2014.

CURSES AND WONDERS

First edition. November 29, 2014.

Written by Mary Catelli.

Dragon Slayer

Ahead, the hills had been burnt black. The fields behind them, even the road underfoot, showed the island's earth was naturally brown, and not a dark brown, either.

The dragon's fire must be hotter than any blaze he had ever seen, Baudouin thought. He drew a deep breath. The air from the hills smelled, faintly, of ash.

A wasteland, he thought, as stark as any in any tale—but then, he was in a tale: a prince of the Sea Folk, delivering a beautiful lady and her lands from a dragon. The Lady Solange had even granted him her favor. The veil bound to his arm was a simple, green with a few leaves embroidered in white, and Lady Solange had looked sour when she bound it on, but the dragon's depredations, and the failures of other knights, must have borne hardly on her.

His guides had grown troubled since the first black scars on the greenery had become visible. Now, though trees and brushes stood to both sides, in full growth, their horses rolled their eyes in contagious worry. Finally, Baudouin said, "You have guided me to the dragon's lands. The duchess did not expect you to bring me further."

One guide said, "She wants us to bury the folk at the farm."

"Along this way," said another. His horse snorted, and he patted its neck. Baudouin thought, briefly, of suggesting that they leave the horses behind, but he had no idea how much further they would have to go.

They came around a bend, and a chimney stood before them, blackened. The house had no other traces.

"How many were there?" said one man, sourly.

"Six. Let's see if we can find them all."

Baudouin's gaze went over the burnt fields. Ashes lay around two skeletons, near the road. Neither could be recognized—both had been so burnt that there was little even of the bone, and that bent by the heat—but one was tiny, no more than a baby. His stomach lurched. His horse pranced, and he collected himself to dismount. He wondered that any legend ever spoke of a knight on horseback slaying a dragon. He patted its flanks and said, "Before you bury, I will be off."

The leader nodded. "Your supplies, then."

Baudouin grimaced as they heaped food and water and blankets on him. The weight bore down on him—but Lady Solange had insisted, and who would refuse a lady's request?

"And there is the dragon's mountain."

Baudouin followed the guide's finger to the hill, standing higher than the rest. He glanced over the distance. And, he conceded, he might need the supplies.

The barren ridges were not safe, he knew. The dragon could swoop down on him as if he were a cow. He walked along the slopes, on the coarse black stone, where he could not be so easily spotted and picked off. The dragon could give him a fair fight, at its lair. But he kept an eye on his distance from the heights. He could not go too far down into the valleys and lose all chance of checking his progress, when the hills had all been burnt to the same black, without trees or houses to mark them.

Baudouin climbed the slope quickly to check again. The dragon's mountain loomed ahead of him. He scrambled back down and walked on. The pack shifted its weight, and he fiddled with the straps, to make it lie more evenly. He had to shed this before he fought the dragon. He wondered if knights had perished for not being swift enough to do so.

He plugged on. The stone grew slicker, as if the dragon had breathed more hotly on it, or more often. His foot slid a little as he came down a slope, and Baudouin walked more slowly. The rise ahead of him glittered in the sunlight, like a glass mountain from a fairy tale. The ridge hid the dragon's mountain from view. Baudouin dragged in a deep breath. The air was almost scentless, carrying only a hint of ash, as if everything burnt had been borne off by the wind. Baudouin started to climb. The ground was smooth, but not entirely even. He made out bumps and dips and placed his feet carefully. He had no choice; he had to know where the dragon's lair was.

At the top, he spotted the mountain, directly before him. He looked down the other side of the hill, much stepper than the one behind him. He grimaced, but who would want to go around? He braced himself with his hand to climb over.

His foot slid out from under him. He snatched at anything within grip, but his fingers slid from the glassy hilltop as easily as his foot had. He jolted from one bump to the next down the slope, futilely scrambling for a grip, and finally lay at the bottom, aching in every limb and certain that he had hit every lump in the hillside. He sat up, rubbing his leg. A chilling breeze came down the valley.

It was not as if he could reach the dragon's lair that day, Baudouin thought, resentfully. He would walk around this hill, and then climb again.

He rose to his feet. Just this hill, he reminded himself.

The hills all looked like the first one, gleaming black glass in the sunlight that had taken on a golden hue as evening came. Baudouin rubbed his hand. He could not travel much further tonight, but he had light for a time yet. He thought that the dragon's mountain lay directly ahead again, that he had reached the other side of the slope where he had fallen.

The hill is not as high, he pointed out to himself. He began to climb. The ground held strange scars, rows of curves like a shell's. He wondered how the dragon caused them and, to get over a rise, put his hand down on the slope—and yanked it away again, bloody.

He slapped his other hand to the wound, swearing at the pain, and sat on the ground. Glass, all right, and as sharp when broken as any other. He swallowed. The blood did not ooze through his fingers, as he had feared it would. But, if he climbed on, he could fall on the broken glass ahead of him.

He wondered if the others had died on the glass and not in the dragon's flames. No bones lay here, at least that he could see, but they might have fallen into some hollow and perished there.

He wondered if he could manage to pick out his way by glimpsing the dragon's mountain through the hills, which he had seen only twice since he had fallen. He had to reach it.

He eased his hand away from the cut. Blood still seeped from it.

At least, it's not your sword hand, said an irreverent thought.

The stream babbled, as if it still flowed through a forest, and the air smelled of water. No plants grew on the banks, or in the water, and no fish swam through it, but the water looked clear.

There's not much ash about, though Baudouin, and the dragon's fire might not dry up a spring. Water rippled over the rocks in the stream bottom. The fire could seal a spring off, but water would break through.

His hand ached. Baudouin climbed down to lie on the bank and stick his hand in the waters. The icy touch nearly made him yank it out again, but he forced it back under, and the pain in his hand sank.

The sunlight had turned orange, the eastern sky was darkening, and the west held clouds of red and pink, with the moon a fragile white curve over them. He would not travel much further today. His fingers brushed against a stone. He wondered even how far he had gone. The ridges and valleys crisscrossed in a fantastic pattern, and when he managed a glimpse of the dragon's mountain, it never seemed any closer.

He clenched his sound hand. At least he had not found the stream before. He was not wandering in circles, entirely.

Though the hills had sometimes looked familiar.

As if all dragon-burnt hills did not look very alike. Baudouin sat up. His left hand ached from the chill, but less than it had from the slice. He could not light a fire, not without attracting the dragon, but no animals lived in this waste, to be frightened off. Lady Solange had given him blankets enough to keep warm in any hollow among the stones.

The sliver of a moon had set shortly after the sun, leaving Baudouin in starlight. He wrapped the blankets more closely about himself. The wind had not picked up much, and he had found a sheltered niche, but the air had grown chilly.

His hand hurt.

Light flared on the horizon. Baudouin's gaze went to it: orange flames, leaping up. Then, silhouetted against them, the dragon sprang up, its wings beating the air as it flew off.

Baudouin wondered what the dragon had burned. He looked away, remembering the dead baby, and wondered whom it had killed. He huddled into the blankets and tried to rest, if not sleep.

Every limb protested as he slowly woke in the morning chill. The eastern sky was barely gray, and the sky overhead black, but Baudouin shivered, unable to sleep, and try to rise. Each movement brought new protests; he set his mouth and stood, and then he picked his way down to the stream to drink. The water was colder than the day before, but the stiffness eased. Some.

He ate by its banks as the sun rose and shone on his way, though the shadows it cast were as sharp as knives. Nothing stirred in the wasteland. Not a bird, not a breeze, not a falling rock.

He rose and plodded on, and his legs slowly came back to life. Sunlight glittered off the rock about him, but he could make out the dragon's mountain ahead from the valley as he walked along.

The valley split about a sharp, high mount of rock and veered off in two directions. Baudouin paused. Neither one led straight to the mountain, but the sunlight made the edges of the mountain before him look sharp, and he had no desire to find out the truth the hard way. The ground was uneven to the point of lumpiness, but he made his way along it well enough.

He choose one way.

The sun rose, and the air about him warmed. Baudouin shifted his pack and wondered how far he would have to fare. The mountain had not looked that far ahead, but he did not know how large it was, and distances could deceive. And he still had to get through the hills about it. His head bent as he looked at the ground before him, for footing, instead of eying the mountain, and trudged onward.

The advantage of sacrificing a maiden to the dragon, he thought, was that the dragon would come to get her.

Sweat trickled down his neck. Then, if the dragon were easy to get to, one of his predecessors might have slain it already, and he did want the fame of having slain it. The slope ahead of him rose, and Baudouin climbed. Then, an earlier death would have spared the isle the depredations of the dragon.

The sun beat down on the back of his neck.

I came as soon as I could, he thought. It has ravaged through no fault of mine.

The valley sank again, and a body lay, face-down, in it. Not a skeleton. Intact, even. Baudouin looked at it for a long moment without approaching. Unlike the ones at the farm, this one had not been burnt. Even its clothing was intact, and the sword the man had carried.

With crawling reluctance, Baudouin came over to the body. The land had not even enough free rocks that he could cover the body, but he stood over it and did not move. His gaze flickered over the corpse. The sword marked him out as another would-be dragon slayer, but the body had no visible wounds, not even any cuts such as Baudouin received, and no blood spread from the body. Nor was it charred; the dragon had not breathed on him.

Hunger? wondered Baudouin. Or thirst? The pack seemed to weigh more heavily, and he shifted the straps. With streams in this land, the man could have found water—except that when he thought on it, Baudouin realized that he had not seen or heard another stream, nor so much as smelled water on the air. He did not even know if he could return to the stream he had come from.

He tried to gauge how much longer his food would last. His mind felt numb. He walked on.

Baudouin looked at the stone ahead of him. That rock, the one with the scars like shells—like so many other rocks. But he still thought that the pattern on that one was distinctive enough for him to say that he had seen it before.

His mouth narrowed. If so, he had traveled in a circle for half the morning.

Wind came down the valley behind him, tugging at his hair, carrying a faint scent of ash—and as dry as ash, as well. He had not seen the dragon's mountain in an hour, he had found no other water, and if he could not find his way, he might join that other dragon-slayer and never face the dragon.

He wondered if any dragon-slayer had found the dragon. He ran a hand through his hair, and brought Solange's favor in front of his face. He looked at the veil a minute. A fine knight he was proving, worthy of the honor she had done him.

He had only spent a day in the waste, Baudouin reminded himself. He stood in no imminent danger of death. He could still show Lady Solange that he was worthy of the honor, and could do what all the men before him had failed at.

He let out a long breath. The shadows shifted as the sun rose, and the scene could look altered under the new light. If he wanted to tell if he had been here before, he would have to mark the place. Briefly, he considered the favor, or the blankets, to leave a stripe of cloth behind—but he had been cold enough with the blankets last night, and the favor would not last long, and was a lady's gift to boot.

Somehow, he thought that Solange would not be too offended at such a fate, but, then, the favor would not last long enough to mark out the circle he thought he had traced.

Scratching out a sign on the stone would blunt the sword, and that he had no desire for, but the pommel. . . . He considered the stone before him for a minute. It looked glassy. He drew his sword and considered the steepest part, where it would be easiest to bring the sword to bear. Drawing a deep breath, he stepped up. The stone was unmarred. He would be able to see a pattern clearly. He smashed the pommel against the stone. A little dust flew, and a spider web ran out from the blow, but not, he thought, enough to be visible if he only glanced.

Why am I doing this? he wondered. His mouth was dry, and he stopped to drink before he tried again. For the fame and glory? But I doubt the legend would describe the perils of getting to the lair.

Because you're too stubborn to admit that you had to back down, said one sour thought.

He swallowed, and lowered the bottle. No, that was not it, the dragon still roamed the land, and he had come to slay it. The difficulty of it only increased the heroism of it.

Baudouin considered the stone. He wished that the legends told more of the petty difficulties of slaying the dragon. He put away the water and took up the sword again, to see what repeated blows would do. He had to ensure that he could pick a new path, if need be.

And at this moment, he felt coldly certain that he would need it. But that would mean he would need to make the marks different, so that he could tell them apart. He sighed.

Baudouin looked at the three circular scars like spider webs, on the stone opposite. He closed his eyes, as if not seeing them would deny the difference. This was not the first place where he had marked the stone, but it was close to it. He wondered if he had been mistaken when he first thought he had gone in a circle, but completed the loop not long after.

No time to moan, he told himself. It did not rouse his spirits, but he went back. The path branched a while back, and he could turn there.

The dragon's mountain appeared in a gap between two hills. In the sunset, it glittered scarlet. Baudouin watched the gleam. He had easily walked the distance to it three times over that day, with doubling back and picking of new ways. He might reach there the next day, if the paths were no worse.

But someone would die tonight, under the dragon's fire, because he had not reached the dragon's lair. His stomach churned, and he turned away to camp. He could do nothing now, he reminded himself, however bitter it felt. Others had perished in the dragon's fire when he had not heard of how it plagued these lands, and while he fared here.

He looked at the food as he picked some out to eat. Enough for a handful more days. He considered trying to escape and then return. It would make him look a fool, but he could not bring himself to dismiss it out of hand.

Still, he had a few days' food, and could consider what to do when the food became scarce. He could pick his way out more quickly than he had found it in. He looked at the bread and cheese. If the legends told how fame and glory were gained, few young men would aspire to be heroes. He had guessed right that morning: he did not wish to retreat because he was stubborn.

"'Fickle as water, you shall not excel,'" Baudouin reminded himself, and ate. The wind was already growing cold.

The noon sun shone overhead, and Baudouin plodded wearily on. He had tried to ignore the dragon's attack last night, but the flames, even higher than the night before, kept returning to his thoughts. He still ached from the night on the stone in the cold. No fame and glory was worth this. He glared at the stones underfoot. The dragon's mountain was drawing closer—he had seen it past the last turn—but the footing was growing worse. "I wonder. . . ."

His grumble stopped in mid-word as he stared at the indentation that made the ground so lumpy. They were not random, but had a common shape: three enormous toes off a central foot, and a claw at the end of each toe, digging deeper. He stood over one, and poked the claw hole with his boot. His foot nearly fit within it.

He let out a long breath. He had known the dragon was a fearsome monster. This but confirmed it. He ought to go on. He stood there, his hand hooked on the straps to his pack, and nearly reeled. No, he had lied. He had been told that the dragon was terrible. Now, he knew.

His head bent, he walked on.

A stream's babble surprised him. Once again, the air smelled of water, and Baudouin hurried forward. The stream was shallow and wide, as if forced out of a narrow streambed by the land's tumults, but when he dropped to his knees and took the cold water in his hands, it was clear. He drank. The taste of it gave no sign that its stream flowed through a dragon's land.

The dragon's mountain loomed ahead. Even at noon, the shadow reached toward him. Not much further, Baudouin thought. He crossed the stream, as it barely rose to his ankles, but stopped on the other side to fill his water bottles. He could hardly tell when, or if, he would return to the stream, or find another. The water nearly had numbed his hands by the time he rose to look for the dragon's mountain again.

It stood ahead of him—along the stream, Baudouin realized, and followed its track without, for once, having to mark the path. The stone about was dark, but the sunlight flashed off the waters, and cast rippling lights over the blackness. He wondered if the stream sprang from the mountain. That would make the journey entirely too easy.

The mountain vanished behind another hill. Baudouin considered the two routes about it: one with the stream running through it, the other as dry as a bone. He did not know that the stream did not spring from the dragon's mountain. Hiking his pack up, he walked alongside it. Here and there he had to wade through the water, and the cold penetrated his boots, but the bank let him walk on it most of the time, and the dragon's mountain emerged from the hills again and again, each time larger, and its shadow reached out to him.

At the dragon's mountain, the stream babbled along its base. Baudouin walked on, looking for any sign of the dragon. Then a sound came through the hills, a sound like a hiss, and another like coins clattering over each other. He could not make them out perfectly, and guessed he had heard echoes and not the original sound. He looked up the mountain. The stone looked as glassy, and uneven, as any he had seen, and he had not seen that the stone he had cut himself on was broken before it sliced open his hand.

He let out a long breath. The dragon, he thought, would endanger him far more than even falling on shards of glass. The sun stood half way to the horizon, again, and Baudouin squared his shoulders. He could not let the dragon raid tonight, if he might stop it. But he stood a minute longer, listening to the wind among the stones. He wondered if any of the others had made it this far, or if they had all died among the stones. He did not think it likely; he had managed his way here himself. The breeze tugged at his hair. That showed, he conceded, that it was not a remarkable achievement.

The pack had become so familiar that he nearly started up the mountain with it, but a strap shifted on his shoulder as he clambered up, beyond the stream. He had been right about it, Baudouin thought, and shed the pack. It would not be wise to face the dragon with that burden.

He picked his way with care through the gullies and ridges and kept as low as he might, to avoid the dragon's glance. The stone was slick underfoot. If he wanted to get down again, he could go as quickly as he had from that ridge, the first day. He walked more slowly as he climbed, but did not stop.

Lights glittered against a stone ahead. Like the light from the stream, thought Baudouin, but golden. He slowed but approached, and the sound of the dragon's hissing breath echoed from the stones. Then the dragon moved, coins clattered too loudly to be mistaken, and a breath of air came toward him, smelling of heat. Baudouin crouched as the golden lights appeared just ahead of him, and crept closer. A cave gaped before him, its entrance larger than a castle's gates, and the cave was a hollow behind it, like a great hall. One that gleamed.

The dragon spread the cave's length. It was longer than the ship he had come on, every inch of its sinuous body covered with crimson scales no bigger than the coins it lay on. It gleamed darkly among the gold, seeming scarcely lighter than the black stone about its lair. Its black tongue licked the air, and Baudouin did not dare move. The dragon rolled over and started counting out coins. Its talons were as thick as Baudouin's wrist, where they joined its paws, but the tips were sharp, and it delicately moved each coin. Its enormous black eyes focused on every coin. "Gold," it breathed. "Every one of them gold. No silver, no copper."

Dragons, Baudouin reminded himself, are softer in the belly than anywhere else—except the eye and mouth, but I have a sword and not a bow. His hand went to the hilt. He remembered, when he first came into the dragon's land, thinking that the dragon could have a fair fight at its lair, as long as it did not swoop on him unfairly, and carry him off.

He remembered the bodies at the farmhouse.

His hand ran over Solange's favor. To get at its belly, he needed to get under it—and without the dragon's realizing what he intended, or it would rear up and out of sword's reach. If he lured the dragon away, over a gully, he could lie under it and stab up. It might crush him in its throes, or drown him in its blood, but it might die. Baudouin swallowed. And he had come to this isle, as he had told Lady Solange, to kill the dragon.

He stared at the stone ahead of him. Even if he died in the attempt, and another came after and dragged back "proof," to claim the glory, the dragon's death would be worth it. He closed his eyes and swallowed.

A frontal assault would be a fair fight. Baudouin ran his tongue over his teeth. A sneaking attack would be as vile as the dragon's snatching him from a ridge—or burning a farm and slaughtering the farmers.

He wondered if any other dragon-slayers had tried. He edged himself up from the stone. Hard to tell among the burnt rock, but some of the shapes, on the hillside, looked vaguely like swords or bones. All along the slope. Some of them might almost have reached the dragon, or their bodies might have fallen.

The dragon's head swiveled around. Baudouin wondered whether it had spotted him, and drew back. Its head snapped over toward him. Even when Baudouin froze, it lifted its head and drew a deep breath.

Get back, said a thought, and Baudouin scrambled out of the hollow. The glassy slope lay before him. Easy to get down, he thought, and leapt down the slope. For a moment, he slid more slowly than he could run, and the air shifted as the dragon started to exhale behind him, but then, with a jarring blow against the nearest lump, he slipped down the hillside, like a fish swimming downstream. Heat roared behind, and he cast an enormous shadow on the rock ahead, lit up as if by a dozen suns. Other shadows fell there, chunks of flying rock—or drops of molten stone.

The rocks rose behind him, blocking the light, but Baudouin could not stop. He bounced from every lump on the hillside until he lay in a shadowed ravine at the bottom, and did not move. Worse than the ridge, he thought, closing his eyes. The stone was cold against his back. If he lay there too long, he would be so stiff he could not move—but he had been lucky that he had not landed in the stream, and drowned before he could rouse himself.

A hissing sound echoed from the stones, but he could not make out any words. With a groan, Baudouin rolled over.

Something lay beside him, on the stone. He opened his eyes. The skeleton had been so burnt that he could only guess, from the charred sword, that it had been human; the bones were few, and misshapen. From the way the remains lay, perhaps the man had fallen here.

This is how dragon slaying can end, Baudouin thought. And this man had not slain the dragon.

He wondered if the man had tried to sneak up on the dragon, or had boldly and fairly faced him. After seeing the stones about the dragon, Baudouin doubted the difference was great.

He rose to his feet. He had come here to kill the dragon. In spite of himself, his mouth twitched—exactly as he had told Solange he had.

He started back up the slope, choosing each step with care. He wondered if the stone had cooled again, where the dragon had melted it. He wondered if he would recognize the rock about the dragon's lair, or if it had shifted when it reformed.

He looked ahead. Golden light shone on the stone. He came here to kill the dragon, and he could neither sneak up on it, nor openly assail it. Both means would only get him killed. He pondered the matter a moment. If the dragon left tonight, as it every other night, he could hide in its lair then. If it did not notice the shifting of its treasure, he might get a chance to strike before it saw him.

Inglorious, said a faint thought, but vanished before he could dismiss it. It might be the only way he could strike in its lair— but it would mean that the dragon would fly free another night. His mouth tightened, and his thoughts leapt: if he could not strike in its lair, he might succeed if he but got the dragon out of the lair.

"No thieves. . . ."

Baudouin's stomach felt cold. There, the dragon had handed him it. He crept ahead, into the gully. The echoes would carry his voice, and the more confused the dragon was, the more likely it was to lay itself open to his blow. He crouched beneath the stone. The only sign of the dragon was the light glittering from the coins. He drew his sword and held it low in the shadows, lest the dragon make it out by light flashing from it.

Then he glanced about. The gully was narrow enough, he concluded. The dragon could not climb down into it. He swallowed. If this failed, he would have to wait until he could reach its lair in the night, and someone would die.

"No thieves at all," whispered the dragon. "Showed that thief."

Baudouin drew a deep breath and laughed. It sounded blatantly false to him, but silenced the dragon for a minute.

"No thieves. . . ." whispered the dragon again, but its voice sounded hesitant.

"You have to try harder than that," Baudouin said. The dragon hissed but did not move. "Come and get me, if you wish to be free of thieves."

The dragon hissed like a boiling pot. The coins clattered, as if the dragon were drawing them together. "You juss-st want to sneak into my coins."

"When you leave your gold every night?" said Baudouin. It did not sound taunting to him, but the echoes might have stripped his tone from it, regardless of how he said it. The dragon's hissing rose, and the smell of heated metal filled the air. Baudouin crouched lower in the shadows. His heart hammered, and his mouth was bone-dry. "Why would I do it now, when it will be so much easier then?"

"Can't leave him here," muttered the dragon, and the sounds came, of its claws scrapping over stone. Baudouin fought the urge to rise, to see the dragon's progress, but if he could see it, it could see him.

"Thief," whispered the dragon, coming closer. Baudouin's moments were marked out by his pounding heart. His sweaty hand tightened on the hilt. The dragon's nose edged out over the gully, and then its head extended. Against the black, its crimson glowed. Baudouin waited, every muscle taut for the moment when it would go over the gully and leave its belly bare.

But it did not move.

He did not dare move and draw its eye. It had not heard his heart or his breathing, or the gully would be a stream of flame, but tempting fate was folly. The dragon inched forward again, raising his hopes, and then stopped.

Moments stretched by, and it did not move.

Baudouin looked to its head, and then to its neck. Not part of its belly, and no legend said their throats were weak, but the scales looked smaller to him.

And what else was there to do? Wait until it spied him?

If you slice its throat, countered another thought, it will breath fire on you—through the hole, if nothing else.

His hand tightened on the sword hilt. He had thought that this might kill him. He surged forward, his sword rising, to plunge the blade in. It struck the resistance of the scales, and he put his weight behind it again, fighting to cut before the dragon could rise up, and then the blade sliced into the dragon's throat, and the dragon gurgled in blood. Scarlet blood flowed from the wound, splattering Baudouin's hand. It burned, and he hissed from the pain and pulled back. The sword slid with him, and blood gushed from the wound. Fiery hot, it flooded Baudouin's hand. He screamed and staggered back, too much in shock to release the sword, and the dragon thrashed beside him. Farther, said a woozy thought, before it crushes you, and he fled as fast as he could in the pain, staggered off with the thunder of the dragon's writhing echoing behind him and shaking the stone underfoot. His feet tangled with a dip in the stone, and he went down, into a corner of rock. His burnt hand jarred the stone, and he screamed again, unable to stop, drowning out the sound of the dragon. He started to rise, and the anguish in his hand sent him back down, emptying his stomach.

The water bottle struck the rock, and Baudouin grabbed with his sound hand. The water had been cold, hadn't it? He yanked it clumsily open, and splashed his hand.

Blood washed away with the water, and he could see the burnt hand that had lain beneath it. The pain sank, a little. He glanced back. The thrashing dragon might still roll this way, but he could not go on in this agony. He poured the rest of the water over his hand, and the pain sank enough for him to get the other water bottles. He looked at his sword. The blood had eaten into it and left jagged pits in the metal. He held his hand over the metal and let the water flow from the hand to the sword. The blood came off, but the sword would never be the same; in places, he could see through it.

It had done its duty, thought Baudouin. He breathed a sigh of relief. It need not do it twice. He looked back. The dragon was not moving as before, and blood had started to fill the gully.

Go down to the stream, he thought, and stick your hand in the water. You can return later, and confirm its death.

His hand throbbed, and he hurried, despite the danger of falling.

He reached the valley on his two feet, and the stream flowed in front of him. He dropped to his knees and thrust his hand into it. The pain lessened, but did not vanish. With the dragon's blood washed off and the agony not so blinding, he could see the injuries. He might never use the hand properly again. But the quest he had come to perform he had performed. Baudouin smiled a little and sat back, careful to keep his hand in the water.

He could follow the stream, he realized. It had to lead from the dragon's lands, sooner or later, and into Solange's land. Even if it reached the sea, he could walk along the shore until he found his way out.

In spite of his pain, his smile deepened.

The first time the dragon had not struck, Solange had waited up the long night for the news, staring at the stars, each hour fearing the delay meant the dragon had something worse prepared than she had feared the hour before.

Rumors had spread all that day. Exhaustion had forced her to bed, but she had not slept well. Still, when the dragon had not struck for a second night, even she had been infected with the glee, and had walked the streets with a lighter step. She had responded to all questions with the sedate answer that they would not know until someone had seen the dragon dead, but she had been unable to keep from smiling.

She had tried not to hope too hard, she told herself again and again that Prince Baudouin was yet another brash young man, and if she put her faith in him, he might yet betray it. The dragon's disappearance was heartening, but Baudouin could have wounded it, so that it would return in greater fury.

She had not brought herself to dampen anyone else's cheer with these thoughts.

The third day, Solange heard the rumors in the streets, even from her balcony. Not that she could make out the words, but the sibilant excitement could not be hidden, and she came down from the castle to search it out. The first half dozen passersby were excited but unknowing as she, but then she saw a crowd pressing toward her from the city gates. She stopped.

In the midst of it walked a filthy, ragged man, his face marked with pain, his blond hair hidden beneath ash. Solange let out a long breath. If Prince Baudouin had not been the only man to go after the dragon in a month, she might not have known him. She looked him over. Her favor was no longer tied to his arm, but wrapped around his sword hand. A bandage, she guessed, and her heart hammered.

He raised his head to look at her. He did not smile, but his face eased a little. His left hand went to his belt and drew his sword. The metal was dull and pitted. He dropped to one knee before her, and threw the sword at her feet.

"Your true and loyal knight, my lady. He has done the quest he sought to do for you." Solange swallowed. "Do with him as you will."

She drew a deep breath, and put her hands about his wrist to draw up his bandaged hand. He watched her. She brushed the favor, gently, with a kiss.

The Book of Bone

Clearwater looked as if no one would go to law over it—certainly not for years. Rain soaked the fields and filled up the ditches, with not even a breeze perturbing its fall, leaving every inch dull and dreary beneath leaden skies.

Avice, ready to hug herself with glee, watched it from the window. Even when the justice had decided the suit, she had not really believed that her father would settle Clearwater on her, whatever he had promised—but she had held the papers in her hands. Despite raindrops smearing her view, she could not look away from her fields.

Someone stood there.

She blinked. Whoever that was, she had not seen him walking over the field, though she might have missed such a dark shadow—she scowled. Who would walk about in this drenching rain? To stand in the mud?

The figure swept the air with one arm. Light flooded from his hand. Her breath rushed out. The man wore a wizard's robes and cast spells—on *her* lands. "What the devil's that?"

"Really, Avice," said her father, from talking with his man of business behind her, "the language—"

The wizard gestured again. Avice ran, past her father, toward the door. A chilled, damp gust greeted her, and she ran into the driving rain.

Within strides, the cold water had soaked her. Her skirts weighed like lead, and mud clung to her shoes, slowing her. The wizard still gestured. Chanted, too, perhaps; she could not hear in the rain.

I will never reach him in time, Avice thought, but slogged on, her skirts slapping at her legs. His hands did not stop. She could even hear words, despite the drumming rain.

The wizard, a lean, brown-haired man, looked at her as she neared him. He flourished a bone-white staff at her. "You think the king's—justice ended the dispute! This will show you otherwise!"

Avice lunged toward him and grabbed his bony arms. For a moment, her fingers caught the cloth, but he twisted away. She dug in her fingers, trying to keep her grip, but her foot slid on the mud. The cloth and arm slipped free, and she fell, hard, to the ground. She fought for breath. Water seeped into her clothing, and staring blankly at him, she tried to struggle up.

Silently, the wizard vanished. From his hand, the staff fell to the earth.

He *had* appeared out of nowhere, one thought said, with insane clarity. She staggered to her feet. Rain fell on her, sending rivulets through the mud on her skirts.

The staff lay, startling white on mud and grass, and she stared at it for a long moment, seeing odd nubs and dips, before it slowly came her that it was not a staff, but a bone. Feeling numb, she took it up. It felt like any other bone—a leg bone, she thought, but it might be either man or beast.

She plodded back toward the house. Puddles spread to either side, and the ditch was half-full, with circles spreading from every heavy drop that hit the waters. She could not manage half the speed that she had, charging at him. Her arm and side ached, where she had fallen, and she started to shiver.

At the house, she pulled the door shut behind her, to stand, dripping and muddy, on the floor, and be vaguely glad it was of stone. Her father looked grave as he studied her, coldly. Feeling stupid and futile, she looked down. She was colder than she had thought; her hands were the same shade as the bone.

Then, she had retrieved more than the bone. "Lord Blondell," she said. She laid the bone on the table and put her hands about her hair to wring out the water. It splattered on the floor, and she thought of a fire, and dry clothes, and hot drinks.

Her father's eyebrows went up. "That was not Lord Blondell."

"He cursed Clearwater," said Avice, enunciating each word, "he said so, and that Lord Blondell hired him."

The man of business looked away.

"If we lay the charge on no better evidence," said her father, "the king will accuse us of a private war."

Avice stood still, her hands still tangled in her hair. Unlike her sister Mirabel, she would make no grand match—even with lands, she did not have the beauty to attract one—but she could avoid living on Mirabel's charity as an old maid—or could have. If her lands could support her instead. If they were not under a curse that would blight them. She glanced between the men. No one would hire a wizard for a lesser curse than that.

"It would cause trouble, such a charge," said the man of business, his voice gray and neutral.

Heaven help me, Avice thought.

Sunlight shone over where the wizard had stood. All about it, grass grew lushly green, and bees buzzed over sweet, bright wildflowers, but within, yellow grass lay on the ground, as if scythed, in a perfect circle. When the dew vanished again, it would be as dry as—her mouth twitched—bone.

The circle spread. The bounds already touched the house; roses bloomed, red, yellow, and pink, against the walls, and sweetness hung on the air, but the bushes nearest the curse had withered to brown.

The roses were among the great charms of Clearwater, blooming all summer long. She had liked that tale even when she was a small girl and knew nothing of lands.

Avice bounced a peasant baby on her hip; he gurgled merrily enough.

"My lady, what'll happen to us?" his mother said.

Avice swallowed. She had tried; she had gone to stop the wizard and defend them all, with only her bare hands at that.

"I do not know, but—" She gestured at the carriage her father had ordered. "We go to ask a scholar to break the spell. Master Clement. He is a master of magical learning. And we can go and return in a day."

She closed her mouth before she talked of what a pest she had had to be before her father would agree. As if he had not believed she would persist when her lands were at stake.

In Master Clement's study, sunlight slanted in from half dozen windows, most of which were half-covered by bookcases and stacks of tomes, and dust motes drifted, gilt by the light.

Avice sat with her hands folded in her lap, and her ankles crossed. Her father described the wizard's attack; she could not fault him for accuracy, only indifference.

"A bone wizard, Lord Harding," said Master Clement, plump and brown and fussing with his papers. "Very rare. I can't imagine finding another to consult with. There is a book, the Book of Bone. . . legendary for its learning on it. . . but you will need the knowledge now. . . ." He shuffled through more papers, frowning.

"Do you know how to break the spell?" her father said.

"Ah no, Lord Harding. Only that breaking the bone will not do it." The scholar shuffled his papers. "You had best find the Book of Bone."

He sounded, Avice thought, doubtful of the possibility. "What is this Book of Bone?"

Her father scowled, but the scholar peered at her. "A book. On bone wizardry."

Her father rose to his feet. "Thank you for your time."

"An honor, Lord Harding, Lady Avice."

Avice's hands tightened about each other. "There are other scholars," she said.

Like an owl trying to make sense of day, Master Clement looked at her. Her father scowled again, but the scholar, oblivious, said, "I do not know of any who have made a study of bone wizardry, any more than of bone wizards themselves."

Which he had not said to appease her father, but still she said, "Do you know where I might learn of them?"

Her father snorted. "You think you learn more of scholars, in season, than Master Clement has in a lifetime? What do you think you can do?"

Avice thought of scholars, libraries, and then— She stood. "I will appeal to the king."

Her father eyed her. After a minute, he said, "How can you? How will you travel? Where will you stay?"

"I will use my allowance and stay with Lady Witt." Avice smiled. "My dear godmother has invited me to visit her before, and said I could come at any time—to match-make, to be sure, but I must look to my dowry for that."

Master Clement looked between them with mild eyes, but her father spat out his words, as if Master Clement were no more of a witness than a cow would be.

"Looking to your dowry? Babbling wild charges? When there are a thousand curses in this kingdom?" He stopped to draw a breath, and his voice was laced with malice. "I can't stop you, but you will go *alone*. I will not permit you to take a maid." He glanced sideways. "And it is unkind of you to argue so in the study of a scholar, disturbing his studies."

"Then," said Avice, "you should permit me to ask my questions in peace, and so not waste his time in our quarrels."

"Lady Avice," said Master Clement. "Your father is quite right. The king does not deal with petty curses, laid between neighbors in minor quarrels. As for other scholars—you saw how you had to travel to me. How could you travel to the wastes and forests where many of them live?"

"Many of them live in towns," said Avice.

"Not the ones who seek strange knowledge—and bone wizardry is strange indeed."

Her father eyed the door. This time, Avice went.

As the carriage rolled over the roads, it passed wheat fields, orchards that grew green between the blossom and the fruit, pastures where sheep grazed—peasants tending them. It looked very like Clearwater, where she was lady. Her duty was to preserve those fields, pastures, orchards, and peasants, and without them, she would be a poor and ragged relation, lucky to have a godmother or sister to take her in.

She felt as cold as when the rain had drenched her. She folded her hands in her lap and tried to work out what she would need to pack. A gown for court itself would not be needed.

Shocked though she had been, Lady Witt had been willing to aid her. Her dowry had to take precedence over attending a court function.

Avice walked down crowded streets. Sunshine gleamed on the way, all about, but even though she was one, she did not stare like a country chit. The palace loomed, the white stone set with a thousand windows. Banners in green and violet and gold flapped by the hundreds beneath the puffy white clouds.

The front gates were black wrought iron adorned with gold, and had soldiers in green uniforms on guard. There, a flock of ladies, glittering in gems and golden satin, entered. Avice kept her hands from smoothing her plain blue skirt and dragged her gaze from the great gates. The serious business was conducted through the back doors. She sighed. Especially if you were no courtier.

She walked along the cobblestoned way. The crowds about her soon grew more soberly, and cheaply, clad. Here and there some official strode, sumptuous in red velvet or blue satin among the underlings, or some messenger in brightly trimmed livery.

The castle proved larger even than it looked; she had to walk almost as far about it, in this crowd, as she had to reach it, but around the final corner, she picked out her door. It did not look like much, no more than a side door at Clearwater would look, but Lady Witt had known where to appeal. There, the guard, less grand than those by the front gate, directed her to a servant, in the royal livery of blue and gold, who led her inside.

Narrow though they were, with low ceilings and stairs of cast iron, the white-washed corridors bustled: people in livery, in uniforms, in drab attire of clerks, or dressed as gentry; petitioners, officials, courtiers; gossiping, arguing, hunting through papers, debating points, and rushing through the warren of rooms and corridors as if it were a straight path. Her own guide walked steadily, without glancing back. For fear of losing him, Avice did not dare hesitate.

Snippets flew by her, of names and places she had never heard of, of curses and sorcery and all sorts of magic. One named her and bone wizardry, and another wondered how much the curse had cost, but even then she could not hesitate. She scurried down a short stair of three steps, following her guide into a new corridor, and around a corner.

There, the servant stopped. Avice blinked with surprise. So she would not wander forever in a maze, devoid of a center, both inextricable and impenetrable. And the corridor they were in was, for once, empty of all other people.

The servant opened a door and bowed. "Lady Avice of Clearwater." Then he darted off, lost past the corner, even before she had a chance to look inside. She drew a deep breath, reminded herself that fleeing would ruin all she had done to get this far, and inched forward.

The windowless office behind held more papers than Master Clement's study, in a far smaller space, with heaps so large that they might stand on the floor, or on a hidden desk in places, but none of the papers were musty with age, or even yellowing. One desk was clear, and from it, a lamp lit the room, and a middle-aged man, his fingers ink-stained, surveyed Avice—Sir Mark, she thought, and curtseyed—and two young men stood by the wall.

He finished his survey, giving no hint of his thoughts, and turned to the men. His voice was drab and uninterested.

"Justin, Matthew, this is Lady Witt's goddaughter. I told you of the curse."

One of them, a small, dark man, looked at Avice with bright curiosity. Avice felt her face heat.

"Should we return later?" asked the other, a blond, lean man—handsome, but rather cold. He did not look at Avice.

"No, Justin." Sir Mark looked at Avice again. "Lady Witt did not particularize. You may be needed."

He did not sound as if he thought that probable.

Feeling like a clerk, or a peasant lass delivering a message to her betters, she told her tale. Matthew looked concerned, but neither Sir Mark's nor Justin's faces changed.

"A bone wizard, then," Sir Mark said, "but not powerful."

Avice gawked. The curse would ruin Clearwater—

Her face must have been clear enough, because he raised an eyebrow. "Lady Avice, a dangerous bone wizard could have laid Clearwater bare that day."

"But, sir, Clearwater *is* being laid bare."

Sir Mark sat back and steepled his fingers together. "Yours is not the only curse in the land. Far from. The law does not concern itself with trifles, and the king can not send men to deal with every petty piece of malice."

Avice faltered. She summoned up the memory of withered grass, of the fields that were laden with wheat—now. Her thoughts twisted. "An ignorant bone wizard might have laid the curse so that it would spread past Clearwater."

She had not thought it possible to convey even less interest in his tone. "Do you know how much effort your paltry little curse would take? When there are far more destructive ones raging?" He looked at his papers. "I will present your case to the king."

Avice opened her mouth and shut it again. She glanced aside. Justin was impassive. Matthew looked indignant, but unwilling to intercede. Avice's shoulders slumped. Or, perhaps, unable to. In the king's service, so young a man would have to obey his elders.

Lord, she prayed, with your justice endow the king, and with your wisdom, the king's son—but she felt leaden.

"I could show Lady Avice to the door, sir," Justin said, coolly, without a glance at her, "so we do not have to summon a servant."

And wait for one, thought Avice, bitterly. She wondered what they did that they did not want her to overhear. She could not even blackmail them with secrets, not when they were in the royal service, and the king's secrets.

"Do so," said Sir Mark, without looking up. He started to sift through one pile.

Matthew bowed. "A pity we could not aid you, Lady Avice."

His face impassive, Justin offered her his arm. Avice let him lead her into the corridor. She found it hard to walk steadily. He led her through the crowds, down a back stairway that was empty as they went down. It was so narrow he went before her; he glanced up.

"Lady Avice, the king will not deem the curse important." His pale hazel eyes caught her gaze. "If he would, we would then go to the Great Library, for the Book of Bone. We would need it to master the bone wizardry involved."

The Book of Bone. First Master Clement had recommended that, and now she knew where to look—Avice swallowed and continued down the stairs after him. The alternative was her father's telling her that he told her so, and Mirabel's charity. The knowledge had fallen into her path, and it would be folly on her part to ignore it.

At the door, Justin bowed courteously, and turned away as if to dismiss her forever.

She shivered and stepped into the sunlight's warmth. An urchin ran by her. And, she thought, the alternative for the peasants would be the life of a vagabond.

First, she had to persuade Lady Witt that she could not just stay at court—she hoped the woman would not believe she could wangle her a grand match, but reminding her that preserving her lands was a noble's duty would help—and then for the road.

Flags flapped in the wind, and it tugged on her hair and her skirts. First of all, she had to return to Lady Witt's.

Carts clattered along. Avice walked back down the street. Two drivers, one of a carriage, began to bellow at each other. Her mouth twisted, and then it struck her: if she arranged for her journey before she spoke to Lady Witt. . . she walked faster.

Days of carriage riding left her feeling stiff, but she had no need to wait. Down the street, lined with majestic oaks. . . trying not to look like a country chit again. The street held crowds, many dressed as travelers in a crowd of merchants and farmers, laborers and vendors hawking sausages or handkerchiefs, but her gaze went on ahead.

Four stories tall, the ivy-covered library towered over the street, and even the oaks. People emerged from the crowd to stream in or streamed out and mingled with the street again. Most of the travelers went that way. Avice walked closer, and the air smelled of sweetness: on both sides of the entranceway, roses bloomed red and white. Few even glanced at them.

Avice gave them no more than a glance herself before she joined the flow. Unlike the court, there was no guard standing or need for petition, or even a line of those waiting. Light-hearted, she hurried up the pale marble stairs and into the main chamber, as tall as the building. Round, the chamber was capped with a dome made of glass, letting in green-tinted light. On each floor, the walls were pierced, showing the shelves filled with book after book after book.

Avice gulped and looked down. In the polished marble of the floor, a labyrinth was depicted. Inlaid dark stone traced folds more intricate than any labyrinth she had ever seen before.

How fitting, she thought, raising her head. People intent on their paths eddied about her. She had no time to hunt, but across the floor, a librarian stood in the ash-brown robes. She crossed the labyrinth to him and asked where she might find the Book of Bone.

The man stared at her. After a moment, he scurried over to an archway; there, he spoke to another librarian, at a desk, intently. Avice drew a deep breath. She could not have been the only traveler to ask for a book. Still her hand clasped and tightened on the fabric of her skirt.

The woman at the desk rose and came toward her. Her hair was the same ashen brown as her robe; her eyes were dark and calm and brown, like a forest pool steeped with oak leaves.

She inclined her head, courteously. "May I ask your name?"

"I am Lady Avice of Clearwater."

The librarian nodded. "A moment, my lady."

Minutes later, Avice stood in a small, whitewashed room, her heart hammering from the climb, and wondered if news of her had arrived before she did. Three flights up, tucked away in a

corner of the library, the room was quiet. Sunlight lit it—
greenly, because the light came through the ivy over the window.
It held two chairs, but she could not bring herself to sit. A breeze
stirred the leaves over the window, and she walked over and tried
to look out. The gaps in the leaves showed bits of the crowds
bustling below.

Her tongue touched her lip, and she reminded herself that
they had not told her that they did not have such a book.
Perhaps—perhaps with books of such power they needed to
fetch them from behind locks and bars. Or to verify that she was
whom she claimed to be. She swallowed. The curse itself showed
the need for care.

Footsteps sounded on the corridor, behind her. Avice turned.

Another librarian nodded to her. Though he still stood
straight, his face was lined, and his hair and beard were white.
"Lady Avice of Clearwater? Seeking a book?"

She straightened, feeling like a small child. "Seeking the Book
of Bone." And closed her mouth before she prattled.

The librarian gestured to a chair. Avice perched on its edge.
He did not take the other chair.

"I fear. . . there is. . . ." His hand clutched at air. Moments
inched by, and her heart hammered harder than when she
ascended those stairs so swiftly.

After a minute, he shook his head. "Lady Avice, I will show
you the Book of Bone."

Avice rose, feeling icy.

He led her down several halls, opened a door and revealed a
book-lined nook. His face tragic, he took one tome and held it
out, open, to Avice. Her stomach curdled, but she looked down:
blank pages. She took the book in hand and flipped through it.
For a minute after, she stood with it. Was it some jest? That
nothing was known, so someone created a book with nothing in?

The librarian lifted it from her hands as gently as if it were a
newborn lamb and looked at it with sorrowful eyes.

"It, too, is under a curse. An older one than that on your lands." He closed the book, softly. "Once upon a time, someone, some wizard, came for a book— " He gestured about. "—and a librarian refused him. The wizard cursed the books, since if they could not be read, it made no difference why not."

Avice's tongue felt heavy in her mouth. She forced it to move. She had come this far. "Was there no condition on the curse?"

He shook his head. "Or we have not heard it. He died a century ago; no man has ever broken it on any of these books." He sighed heavily. "We have tried to replace them with good copies, but some we have not found. This is one." He turned to slide the book back in as if it were still precious and useful. Perhaps it was to him; perhaps he had dreams that someday, the curse might break.

Avice closed her eyes. The librarians would have broken that curse, if they could have. They had a library with many tomes about magic, and wizards consulted them, so the librarians could set such a price on reading their books, if any of them knew such a spell.

She swallowed. Then, perhaps none of them felt the urgency that she did.

"The—" Her mouth moved like the cogs of a mill when the mill pond offered only a trickle of water. She swallowed. "The king's men said they would come for this if they needed to break a piece of bone wizardry."

His eyebrows went up. "They would fare no better than you," he said, with a new crispness to his voice. "The king himself would fare no better. Nothing can be done."

She managed to wonder if the actual encounter might perhaps happen differently, but she felt too dispirited even to be waspish.

She wondered if the king's men might know of other means to break the curse—and doubted that they would yield such knowledge for the asking. She followed the librarian as he went down the stairs. It occurred to her, in the third coil, that he had found the book readily. He had known it was one of the cursed ones.

The railing slipped upward, through her fingers, as she descended and pondered how many people had come, seeking help. Enough so that they kept it in memory.

She stood on the marble floor again, and looked at the doorway.

"I will stay and look for knowledge on curses," she said.

"My lady?" He turned his head to look at her. "For the bone magic curse, you will not find the knowledge outside a book of bone magic. If that one—" He gestured upwards, toward the arched entranceway. "They have searched every book for a cure."

She drew her breath in—the air was scented by flowers growing outside—and let it out again. "Perhaps they did not search for where else they could search. Perhaps they did not have the means to search through the kingdom for a cure."

The librarian raised an eyebrow. She looked back. They could turn her out if they wanted, but until then, she would search.

"What harm could I do? I can not curse those books again."

Outside the library's kitchen was not far from the clatter of pots and pans, but the servant there still whispered.

"That librarian—" The servant glanced at Avice. "He was glad. His books were safe—from anybody. Never told nobody how to break it."

"There was a way?" Avice's heart pattered faster.

"Course there were. Stands to reason."

Avice's heart stopped, then settled to a normal beat. Why had she expected this to be different? She had heard the curse was placed by an angel, a fairy, or a wizard; she wondered, even, whether the story was true. Whether perhaps it had been the idle, unintended consequences of some other spell, or a librarian had cursed the books to keep them out of the hands of an evil-doer and lied about it.

She, at the moment, could imagine far more tales to explain the curse than ways to learn how to break it.

She thanked the servant and walked toward the library's front door. The roses still bloomed, and her mouth twisted. She had looked closely enough now to see that the white and red coloring was often white petals speckled with blood red.

A few souls had even told her that the roses had been planted after, to tear to pieces anyone who came to curse. Too late to do her any good.

She walked through the sweetness. Back to her first notion: more scholars. Her steps slowed. Or to stop the search. If the curse spread from Clearwater, the king would have to stop it, and if it did not—other women lived on sisterly charity.

She climbed the stairs and thought of her defeated return, of her father's scorn, of her sister's mirth. It did not seem so horrible, and she wavered. She forced herself to remember the blight, to think of the fields withered, and the peasants thin with hunger.

She walked into the Great Library; now familiar, she picked out a side door. All about the room, the librarians ceased to catalogue books as they looked at her. She had turned into a legend, she thought sourly.

"Lady Avice," said one. "You have had no good fortune?"

"No. I will leave this city." She drew a deep breath. "I intend to seek out scholars on how to break either curse."

They murmured their gratitude.

"It might be useful if I might show them the cursed book."

The librarians' faces went blank. One drew a deep breath, as if readying herself to speak.

"Or you could keep it here. Safe. As safe as the librarian kept it."

Avice woke in the inn's bed, her face buried in the goose-feather pillow, the sheets coarse about her. Noise from the courtyard drifted in. Her hand slid under the pillow to touch the Book of Bone. After two months and seven scholars, neither curse had been touched. Her hand tightened on the spine.

"I'm no worse off than I was before, then." Her voice was firm, but she did not convince herself.

Gray morning seeped around the shutters. She rose. She had a scholar to speak with. Then, whatever he knew or did not know, she would have a trip to take, and only which coach she had to take would change.

She opened the shutters, letting in the daylight. Below, beside the willows, travelers gathered about the coach. A girl scattered grain from her apron to clucking chickens.

Avice sighed. God help me, she thought. She went to comb out her hair.

A colorless voice came from the doorway. "Lady Avice, wash water."

"Come in."

The drably clad maid obeyed, laid the bowl on the stand, and started to leave. A hesitation in her steps caught Avice's attention. She swept about, and the maid's hand was under the pillow. At Avice's glance, a guilty expression leapt on her face.

"Thief!" Avice grabbed the maid's wrist. Her half-braided hair spilled loose. "Thief!"

Voices arose below, querulous, questioning. The maid yanked against her grip, and nearly wrested herself free. Avice raised her voice again. "THIEF!"

Voices changed to angry clamor. The innkeeper, poker in hand, charged up the stairs. Servants and guests scrambled after him, and shouted and exclaimed every step.

"Wasn't!" said the maid. Avice shook her arm; the maid cringed and sputtered, "He said, he said."

"What did he say, Ida?" the innkeeper said, his lip curling. A big, red-faced man, he loomed over the maid. Avice's grip loosened.

"He said—he said it was his book." Ida shrank back. "That I touch it—he'd pay...."

"Who was he?" said Avice.

Ida's lips moved but made no sound. Avice felt as if a chilly breeze had touched her back, and stepped backward. Her eyes looking desperate, Ida tried again, forcing her mouth to move, desperately trying to force breath into her words. And then a hollow look came across her face.

The innkeeper slapped her. "You tell our guest who you stole for!"

"I think she's under a bone curse," Avice said. Her voice sounded strangely flat and dry in her own ears. She pulled Ida's arm from under the pillow. In the maid's rough, reddened fingers was a pale chip of bone.

Exclamations abounded. A cloth was found to wrap the bone up safely. The innkeeper hustled Ida out, talking about the magistrate. The crowd followed, despite murmurs and many glances at Avice.

Avice pulled out the Book of Bone and hugged it to herself. The pages were still blank, but if the bone wizard wanted it, the book had to have some value. Her mouth tightened. It might even mean this scholar would be worth more than the others. It had ever been worse when they made her welcome, and were obliging, because they had never helped her in the slightest.

The housekeeper ushered Avice in from the dusty street, to another study filled with books and papers. She had seen so many—she could even recognize some tomes, owned by many scholars, at a glance—but her heart still beat faster as she handed over the letter.

Master Higgins, a plump man with glasses and a fringe of gray hair, read it and looked up. "How strange. Twice in a month to hear of bone magic." He held it out. "I fear I have no more for you than for the other one."

"Other one?" said Avice, taking the letter back. Had the bone wizard laid more curses? If she could find this victim—many hands would make the labor lighter, if not, perhaps, light.

Master Higgins sat back. "A man—a tall, thin man, brown hair. He wore brown robes, like a university student."

Avice felt icy as the scholar went on to say that he knew little more of him. She knew more. The bone wizard had spoken with Ida, but what was he doing at the scholar's?

He started to ramble about how few scholars knew of bone magic, even the Great Library having little, and Avice collected herself. If she could not learn that here, she might learn another thing. She pulled out the book. Master Higgins leaned forward, frowning thoughtfully.

"I went to the Great Library in search of knowledge. They have the Book of Bone. However...." She fanned the pages.

Master Higgins grimaced. "I have heard of this curse." He spread his hands. "I assure you, anyone who knew the cure would know how grateful the library would be. And what fame it would bring him, to undo such a curse. And I have not the hermit's temperament to forego such honors."

Avice thanked him and left, her thoughts returning to what he had said, and her heart pattering the faster. She did not feel much disappointment, not when she had such matters to think on. The bone wizard had come to Master Higgins. She did not see how that could help her, and she could think of many ways that it could harm. But—to hear of him again—

Her mouth twisted. At least it was a change from the dreary and endless journey.

She walked toward the inn, to where the coaches arrived, and her bag still lay inside. This quest had brought no good thus far, but she had more scholars, and the coach would take her from the bone wizard as she went on her way.

True, if she took the coach toward her home, that would also take her from the bone wizard, but there, she could only sit in the corner and sew. No one else would take on the quest.

"The king *should* administer justice for the land," she grumbled. "And the librarians *should* preserve the books. . . ."

What a prig you are, observed a cool thought.

Avice stopped in the willows' shade and drew in a deep breath. Here she would await the coach—whichever coach she took. She recalled the fields, the withered grass, and the anxious peasants, but it was vague and shadowy. Her eyes closed. The bone curse had to be stopped, she told herself—God help me.

Her bags, she told herself. She did not need any fervor for her task, but she did need her bags.

Beneath the willows, the shadows of leaves and boughs were broken by bright flecks of light, dancing with any breeze. Avice brooded. The bag with the book sat on the bench beside her, the strap slung over her shoulder. Her other bag sat at her feet. She kept an eye on the street, where chickens clucked, and once or twice, she drew her feet away from a child's headlong running, but her thoughts were on the wizard.

Then it struck her, why the bone wizard might be after the Book of Bone. Sir Mark might have guessed rightly about his competence. She swallowed, and her hand tightened on the strap. Then, if that were true, she might have spoken truly, also: the curse could spread far beyond Clearwater.

For a long minute, Avice did not move. She did all that she could, she told herself. For weeks and months, she had.

She still felt cold.

The coach had yet to arrive, it was not even in sight, and waiting was all she could do now.

She felt a tug on the bag that held the book, and it yanked her from her thoughts. She looked down, her hands already going out to seize the bag more tightly.

A thing of bone, no longer than her forearm, stood by the bench. Its sharp face held teeth like splinters in its grinning mouth. Its fingers, having sliced the bag open, snatched the book. She gawked and grabbed it as well. The creature pulled the book back, its fingers scoring the leather cover, but it did not wrest it from her hands. She surged to her feet, wrestling with it.

Then it grinned.

All about them, the air shimmered and popped. Light vanished, and the bench and the willow tree. Damp chill surrounded her, faintly lit by a source she could not see, and smelling of stone.

In Avice's shock, the thing snatched the book away.

"What the devil?" said someone behind her. The sharp voice took on a conciliatory tone. "I beg your pardon, sir. The homunculus should not have arrive so as to disturb us, I should not have taken that wizard's magic in trade for mine, or taken more care with its casting. . . Good Lord!"

Avice turned.

Next to a table, lit by a lamp, the bone wizard stood, his face working. A young blond man sat near him, his expression impassive: Justin. Avice felt the blood draining from her face. Whatever had happened at court, to have a king's man *here*? Her breath was low and shallow, and though she felt faint, she could not force herself to deepen it.

The wizard still stared at her. "I go to recover my own by right—and a thief intrudes. . . ."

His hand rose. Three bone creatures, like the homunculus but enormous, emerged from the shadows. Avice stepped backward.

"Take her to the storeroom," the bone wizard said. "I will deal with her later. I must help my guest first."

The needle-sharp claws drew nearer to her, as if ready to rend. Justin sat like a statue, his face utterly unmoved. Her heart hammering, she hurried in front of those hands as they shepherded her away. Behind her, Justin and the bone wizard spoke, their voices low and unconcerned, as if she were indeed a stray sheep.

The giants walked her into a long stone hallway. Windows at either end barely lit it. One closed the oaken door behind them, cutting off the voices.

She was trembling, Avice realized. But—the king—how could he ignore the curse *that much*? To deal with the bone wizard—but the giants did not stop for her reveries, and she scurried. Even if there had been a doorway to escape by, she could not have taken it before the giants were upon her. That the hall held only walls of stone and heavy oaken doors should not have dispirited her.

They passed half a dozen doors before the giants stopped before an ironbound one, with a thick bolt. She swallowed as they drew back the bolt and pulled open the door. Before they could force her, before she had time to look, Avice dashed inside. She cracked her knee on a chest. The door slammed behind her. The bolt crashed back into place.

High windows shed bluish light over a room packed with cases and chests. Avice collapsed on the nearest. Oh God, she thought, trembling, unable to form a more coherent prayer. For a moment, she managed indignation: calling her a thief when stealing from her. But the spark faded. Oh God.

The first panic faded, and she felt nausea rising. She wondered whose land the king wished to blight. And then her thoughts began to tumble over each other, too unclear in her fright for her to remember them.

She had lost track of time when the bolt rattled. Avice forced her breath in and out, and looked up. The slant of the light had changed, but she could not judge how much time had passed. She felt stiff in every limb, but stood. If the bone wizard was careless, she might escape.

The strap of the bag that had held the book slid down her arm. Avice pushed the strap back up. The bag might prove useful again. Perhaps. She had so little that she did not dare forego anything she had.

The door slid open, revealing Justin. Avice gawked. He held out his hand. His voice was sharp.

"Hurry. He wanted to look at the book, he let me leave on my own, but if he learns you're gone. . . ."

Avice hurried to the doorway. Her heart hammered again, and her hands shook. "How did you come here? The king. . . ."

He grinned at her, his face coming alive in an off-center, charming grin.

"When the bone wizard destroyed some legal documents, then he cared."

He strode down the hall. Avice scuttled to keep up, without argument; they could not leave too quickly for her.

"Documents important to a favored courtier. Your visit must have made it known that the bone wizard could be hired."

Avice's mouth twisted. "There were rumors enough—I heard them when I visited."

"Ah, well, the story spread because such an appointment would be noticed." He glanced sideways at her. "As for the storeroom—the king might care about kidnapping." His pale eyes danced with mischief. "And if I assumed he didn't and found I was wrong, I couldn't come back to fix it. Best to assume he would."

Despite herself, Avice smiled.

Justin's smile faded. "Did the Great Library have the Book of Bone? Is that what he has?"

"Yes, and yes."

He grimaced, glancing away from her.

"It's cursed—"

"I've heard of that curse." He sounded relieved.

They turned a corner, to a door larger than the rest; it would not serve as a barn door, but it might well serve for a ballroom.

For all its size, Justin opened it with ease, and it made not much as a creak. In the fresh air beyond, a grassy hill spread downward. Fields and woods spread in the valley. Avice bit her lip. She could pick out no roads.

Justin shut the door, and they fled. Glad that Justin had come here by more ordinary means, Avice glanced back. The building looked like nothing more than a low stone farmhouse, down to the stack of firewood beside it.

Something launched itself from the eaves. Avice saw nothing more than leathery wings before it was upon them, hurling something from skeletal hands. Her hands went up, futilely, as if she could ward the attack off. Justin grabbed her arm, pushing her behind him, and cried out, sharply, in pain, and the creature circled, its shadow spinning on the grass. Avice darted to the firewood and grabbed a log—the largest one she could get her fingers about—before she turned. The creature dived toward her. She hefted the wood and smashed it through the bone creature in its head-long flight.

The creature shattered, a thousand white bits for a moment hanging in mid-air, and then, striking against each other, falling toward the ground.

Avice breathed hard and stood over the fragments, eying them where they lay pale on the green grass. They did not even twitch, but her breath steadied, and she realized that this could not be the wizard's only guardian. Wondering why Justin had not urged her on the moment that the creature fell, she turned to him, her skirts swirling about her.

He had fallen to one knee, his head bowed, and he did not move as she stared. For a moment, her heart seemed to stop; then, it hammered in her chest, as if trying to escape.

She forced her voice to work. "Justin?"

He looked up. His face was contorted with pain, and sweating. The sleeve of his doublet and shirt were torn, and in the tear, a bone chip had embedded itself in the arm.

Avice touched his forehead and felt fever. Already, she thought. The bone had to be enchanted. She looked about—as if she could find an enchanted wildflower that could heal him, she told herself, scornfully, but the look was not useless. On the house, more creatures moved; she bit her lip.

"We have to get away," she said, and took his sound arm. Without argument, he staggered to his feet.

God help us, Avice thought, and looked about again. A mass of maples, with ferns thick beneath them, stood on the hill. She hurried Justin into its shadows, where the air smelled of green and earth. The wizard appeared in the doorway. Bone creatures flitted about him, some on the wing, some scurried about his feet and up the wall and over the firewood. Avice shrank back and hoped that the trees hid them.

"They won't get far. The spell bears deadly fever. The bone will turn them to bone." His voice carried, as if he knew they could hear. Justin's hand tightened on Avice's arm as the wizard turned to the doorway. "Go. Find them."

Out of the doorway trundled two dozen giants. Large though it was, each one had to duck its head to avoid the lintel, and they came out one by one, turning a bit because they more than filled it.

Her tongue touched her lips. Justin had protected her from the first attack, and the wizard thought them both under that spell, and dying of fever. They had a chance.

She breathed, "Come."

They faded into the forest, hurrying over the litter of dead leaves. No woodland flowers bloomed on their way, only endless trees and stands of ferns half as tall as she was.

Minutes later, deeper in the woods, she stopped. "We have to get that out of your shoulder, Justin."

Without argument, steadying himself on the closest tree, Justin dropped to sit on the earth. Avice knelt beside him, eying the arm, and wishing that her mother had not thought too much tending the sick below a maiden of gentle birth.

He spoke slowly. "Do you need the sleeves off?"

Avice nodded, reaching for the lacings herself. Justin helped shrug the clothing off, but he hissed with pain as the cloth brushed the chip. Sweat beaded on his lean body. A fine young man, thought an insane part of her mind. Avice angrily dismissed it and drew the knife on Justin's belt, to pry out the bone with its tip.

The chip had barely nicked the skin, she could see most of it, but Avice's best efforts drew only gasps from Justin.

Leaves rustled. Avice started, thinking of a bone creature, and glanced frantically about. A breeze had stirred the branches, but she sat back. She had known the bone chip was enchanted.

Justin looked up. "I can... move, if. . . ."

We can not let those creatures brings us back to wizard, she thought, even if Justin spoke more out of hope than ability. She took up his shirt and doublet and stuffed them into the bag that she had carried the Book of Bone in; the clothes would betray their presence to the bone creatures.

"How far are we from anyone else?" she said. Like a sensible traveler, he carried a water bottle; she pressed its contents on him.

With her no longer poking at the bone chip, and with the rest, the pain eased from his face. "A day's travel," said Justin. He drank greedily and looked up again. "By the road, and in good health."

Avice cocked her head to one side. "Why did the king send you here? Did he expect you to find a way to break the spell?"

"To buy a way." He drank again.

Avice's mouth twisted. What a vile way for the king to deal with an evildoer.

Justin shrugged. "My mother was right, after all."

Avice raised her eyebrows.

"When I entered the royal service, she said I would regret it." He smiled, the same charming, off-center smile as before.

A bone creature rustled through the leaves, its pallor catching the stray light. Avice and Justin froze like fawns awaiting the mother doe. It flew by. Perhaps it had nothing to do with them, but Avice rose and held out a hand to help Justin to his feet, and tried not to notice how heavily he had to lean on the tree and her arm to rise, or to think how useless she would be to help, if he could no longer walk.

The sounds of a giant treading on ferns reached them, and they hurried off. The sound faded again. Trees thinned out, until they walked through a sunlit clearing. At one side a cliff rose, slightly taller than Justin, and a spring bubbled from it. Water flowed outward, across the clearing in a stream, though with stones enough to cross. Avice slipped on one stepping stone, getting her foot wet in the cold water, but they crossed and reached the woods, and the shadows of the boughs, again.

We might get away, Avice thought. The sounds of the giants were fading with distance, behind them.

Justin, breathing hard, stopped. He swayed a little. "Can't. . . ."

Avice stopped, biting her lip, and tried to hold his arm. Her fingers no more than brushed his arm when Justin collapsed, so

quickly she could not even break his fall. Her mind went blank.
In their need to escape, she had managed to ignore the pain in his
face, but now. . . .

Flushed, sweating, he looked up. "They're too close; go on
without me."

"They aren't," Avice said. "You need something to drink."
Before he could argue, she took his water bottle back toward the
stream, and then up its banks. The muddy ground squished and
slid underfoot, and her feet grew wetter than when she had
crossed the stream, but she held the water bottle up to the rock.
Despite the sunlight, making it glitter like diamonds, the water
was icy cold. Her hands were numb and white before it filled the
bottle, and she could turn away with relief and walk back to dry
earth, with her shoes leaving tracks of mud and wetness—and her
feet as cold as her hands, at that.

Leaves stirred, down the stream, and across it. Avice pulled
back, behind a green bush, taking care to be quiet. A giant
lumbered from the woods. Past the cliff, she saw another, still in
the trees.

Clutching the bottle to herself, she returned to Justin. As he
drank, she whispered, "He has to know the book is useless. And,
why would he want it? He is a bone wizard."

"He said," said Justin, "that his spells are not easily broken. I
think he can not break them—he knows too little." He hesitated
for a moment and went on more slowly. "He trades magics with
other wizards—the spell that brought you here was one."

And him to Clearwater. Avice fought to keep from groaning.
He must have made many such trades, to have two at hand and
use them so freely.

"So," she said. "He could break the curse on the book once he
got such a traded spell, if only he knows the right wizard. I have
to get it back. He would be worse. . . ." Her voice trailed off as a
thought struck her: if the bone wizard disenchanted the Book of
Bone, she, too, could read it.

She looked at Justin, but his eyes were closed. He shifted, tried to say something, but could not overcome his exhaustion. His blond hair fell over his face. Avice looked at her grubby clothing, at her battered hands, barely warm again, at the mousy hair escaping from her braids.

More knowledge would make the bone wizard more dangerous, but no one else she could find knew how to disenchant the book. Certainly, even if she learned who this other wizard was, she could not trade a spell for it. She licked her lips, and a bird trilled in the distance. She would have to put all her weight on the wizard's belief that she, too, had been struck down and was helpless.

The wind rustled the leaves. Justin rolled over. Hair fell back from his flushed face. Unless she got the Book of Bone, disenchanted, back, Justin would die. She might save Clearwater some other way, but he did not have the time for anything else to save him.

She had seen how the wizard cast spells with abandon, knowing little of his art. She could expect over-confidence.

Leaves shifted, and light danced over the forest floor. Avice considered how the creatures had moved in the forest. There were only twelve of them, and they had radiated out from the house. She bit her lip. If she and Justin got inside that circle without being seen, they would be safe.

He will be safe, Avice told herself, while I go to the wizard's house.

She touched Justin's sound arm to wake him. He stirred and asked for water. Avice gave him some and told him her plan.

Justin stared at her. For a moment, she feared he would refuse to even try.

Then he said, "I can tell you about the house." He drew a deep breath. "He showed me where he works his spells. He would disenchant the book there."

Avice felt a cold weight in her stomach. Moving Justin would put him in such pain that he could tell her nothing. "Tell me now."

Without a moment for thought, Justin nodded.

Justin steadied himself against the nearest tree as the approaching giant left a trail of crushed fern. Avice drew a deep breath and took Justin's arm. Be with us, oh Lord, she prayed, for we are in trouble and need. "Now."

Justin lurched off the tree. Avice suppressed the impulse to hurry. The giant took one last step. They walked over its path and on through the woods.

Justin slowed, and Avice nearly groaned. "Further," she whispered. He nodded and did not slow again. For a long minute, they inched on. She looked back and saw, to her relief, nothing of the giant. "We can stop."

Justin collapsed beneath the nearest tree. Avice urged the last of the water on him. In moments, his breathing deepened. Avice put the bag aside—it would only get in the way—and rose to her feet, her heart hammering. Justin did not even twitch.

Before she could unnerve herself, she walked off. The trampled ferns filled the air with the smell of greenery and made passage far easier. Within minutes, she found herself at the forest verge.

The building still looked like a farmhouse. Nothing moved across its slate roof—although she did not know how stealthy the bone creatures could be. The door she and Justin had fled through faced her. Avice walked up and tried it.

It was unlocked. Her mouth twisted. The wizard must be certain that she was as feverish as Justin—or confident that other magics, within, would stop her.

She stepped inside, pulled the door shut as quietly as she could, and let her eyes adjust to the dimness.

Or perhaps, she thought, he had sent all his bone creatures after her and not realized what it meant. She had little reason to think highly of his judgment. . . and that meant that some of them, not the giants, might find Justin.

The chilly corridor stretched out ahead of her. Avice walked down the flagstones, and though her footfalls were soft, no other sounds broke the quiet.

She counted off doors, her ears straining for any noise, until she reached the one she wanted. Her hand on the latch, Avice listened, but she heard nothing. She opened the door, breathing a sigh of relief at its silence.

The windowless room was lined with cabinets and filled with books, and with bones, glittering crystals, dried herbs, and feathers of every shade, and their enormous shadows, cast this way and that by golden lamplight, but even in that clutter—the lamp burned on a table next to the Book of Bone.

Avice drew a deep breath. The air smelled of dust, of paper, and faintly, of herbs too desiccated to hold much scent, but she did not take her eyes from that tome. Her heart beat, not faster, but harder, sounding like a drum in her ears, as she took in that it was within grasp. Even—the bone wizard could have already cast the spell, leaving her nothing to do but take the book and flee.

Her heart still hammering, she picked her way through the confusion, keeping her skirt from brushing against anything, until she reached the table and lifted the cover. The pages were still blank.

For a moment, her heart seemed to stop.

Swallowing, she lowered the cover, so that the book did not even twitch, and looked about the room.

Small animal skeletons sat here and there. Larger bones lay on the shelves, in baskets, and in heaps on the floor. Avice wondered, briefly, how the wizard had gotten them all, but she had to hide. One basket, filled with green and blue feathers nearly Avice's height, stood in front of a cabinet varnished red. The basket and cabinet cast enormous shadows over the corner.

The feathers stirred as she ducked behind them. She turned to the room. The light still fell on her face. She crouched. Shadow covered her, and Avice drew a deep breath of relief.

Light glittered through a jar, sitting on the cabinet, half full with bone chips like the ones that had wounded Justin. Avice remembered him, lying feverish in the woods. He could die there, alone, even if she succeeded here, and her teeth worried her lower lip. He would die just as readily with her by him and weeping her eyes out.

She remembered the wizard's arrogant confidence that the curse had felled her, too. Her eyes narrowed. She kept an ear cocked, but loosened the jar's lid.

The sound of footsteps came from the hallway—loud, ringing footsteps, having no need to hide. Avice crouched again. The door opened, and the breeze sent a shiver through all the feathers and candle flames. His gaze fixed on a paper in his hand, the wizard came in, and she fought the urge to pull back. Any motion could draw the wizard's eye. She breathed with care, in and out, knowing she could not hold her breath.

"Little fools, interfering with me." He chuckled, dropping the paper on the table. "But there's no escape from the bone chips. That'll teach them."

Avice's hands clenched into fists.

He pottered about, setting candles on the table and lighting them. After minutes that played on Avice's nerves, he laid open the book to blank pages, pulled out a scroll, and intoned. Avice's fingernails scored her palms. Candles burned down, filling the air with the smell of burnt wax. The wizard's words rolled on, and on. Minutes later, he dropped the scroll, making the candle flames waver in the breeze. ". . .to make hidden things visible!"

His words died in the chamber. Molten wax spilled down one candle. Avice's legs ached. With a sigh, the wizard turned to the book. She rose, to stand against the cabinet. Her legs protested, and her heart pattered from the danger of being seen, but she had to see herself. The spell might not have worked.

The wizard flipped through the pages, and Avice peered through the feathers. The writing was dark.

"What was that?" The wizard looked up. Avice froze, wondering what sound she had made. After a moment, the wizard laid down the book.

To summon the bone creatures, Avice thought. She seized the jar. The wizard jerked about, his eyes widening in surprise. A moment later, his hands flew up to gesture. Avice yanked off the lid and hurled the chips at him. They scattered about his feet, over his clothing, and into his hair. The wizard froze.

"Enchanted, aren't they?" Avice picked her way about the chips, setting her feet with more care than ever before. The wizard's eyes tracked her, but he did not move a limb. She picked up the Book of Bone. The wizard's face contorted, and he lowered an arm, only to hiss as a bone chip grazed his hand.

Once safely away from the chips, Avice darted out of the room and down the corridor. Her footsteps resounded. And then she burst out into the sunlight and fresh air, and down the hill to the forest, with the dead leaves muffling her steps.

Justin still lay beneath the tree, his face flushed. Avice drew a deep breath and dropped to the earth next to him. He stirred but sank down again.

Avice fought to keep her hands steady and rifled through the book. Crabbed handwriting filled it. She bent over to page through it, to read that the bone creatures needed only to be broken to be stopped, but nothing about breaking other spells— only the making of them. If she read them rightly.

Justin muttered. Avice's eyes closed for a moment—at all this, he might yet die—but she returned to the book. She had no other way to try; if this failed her, he would die.

A minute later, she read, "For the breaking of all bone wizardry," and dived into the paragraphs. ". . .Even as fern grows where fern molders, so a curse laid by bone. . . ." Avice's fingers tightened on the page. ". . .laying the bone beneath the root of a living plant shall surely destroy the curse."

Avice snapped the book shut. Put it beneath the root, as the peasants did for some crops—

Ferns, she thought, light-headed. By the tree, a small feathery fern nodded, uncrushed. Her fingers dug into the moist earth, and the roots brushed against her hands. She dug more deeply. Half a dozen roots held until she yanked, and the fern came free, with dark, damp bits of dirt dripping through her fingers. Holding it closely, she turned to Justin. His eyes opened, without focusing, as Avice laid the fern to his arm, the pale roots and the almost black earth, with the fern nodding emerald green above. A chunk of dirt freed itself and dropped to the ground. Avice felt a fool, sitting there, her fingers damp and filthy—but no one would see her—

Justin blinked. "Avice? I—" He sat up. The fern, and the bone chip, slid from his arm. "I'm thirsty."

Avice laughed and could hear how wild her laughter was. "You've been feverish." Before she lost her wits entirely, she scoped up the bone chip and laid in the hole, and then she laid down the fern, to bury it in the roots, to be sure of it.

Only then did she think of water.

In yet another dusty inn yard, Justin handed Avice down from the carriage, with the sky to the west once again filled with rose and gold, though overhead it was not yet dark. She rolled her stiff shoulders.

"Master Justin!" A middle-aged man crossed the yard. His black and gold clothing, trimmed with fur, was a courtier's, with only a few concessions to travel. She hesitated. Many a courtier did not dress so well, even at court; she had seen that much in her brief visit.

"Lord West," said Justin, dryly, not heading toward the doorway. Avice glanced between them, unsure whether to move.

The lord glanced at her. "This must be Lady Avice?"

"Yes," said Justin, even more dryly.

Lord West beamed. "The king was pleased to hear that you know how to break this curse—he sent orders—"

Avice wished that they would wait until morning. She glanced at the inn and bit down a yawn.

Lord West blinked, following her gaze. "But of course you can not stay here, at this uncouth inn, like some churlish beggar. You will be Lord Fitton's guests!"

He gestured across the town, toward the gray castle. Avice's heart sank—the beds at the inn were closer—but she did not protest. Justin, his face as unreadable as at court, offered her his arm, and she took it, thinking she might need the aid. At least, they still had enough light to walk by.

Lord West walked alongside. "His Majesty has ordered that this bone wizardry be treated as so a grave matter deserves. Neither Lady Eleanor nor your Lord Blondell will escape."

Avice smiled thinly.

"And His Majesty wishes you to come to the capital, so that he may honor you."

Wishes, thought Avice, chilled. That was an order. "I have to go to Clearwater, where the bone wizard laid the curse for Lord Blondell—I have to break the curse."

"Yes, of course, in due time...."

Avice hunted for words, but found none before they were at the castle, and Lord West left to speak with Lord Fitton. In the gray stone courtyard, chilly evening breezes tugged at her skirt and hair, and she wondered if all she had done would go to waste.

"Lady Avice." Justin's face was as unreadable as the day they had first met. "Let us talk. In the garden, perhaps."

Avice swallowed and came with him. A bench stood among roses, blooming as colorfully as the sunset; Justin handed her to it.

"The king will insist," he said. "He wishes to honor you."

"It would be folly to defy him," said Avice, sharply. "I am not that much of a country chit."

Justin grinned. "He sent no orders about me."

After a minute where the only sound was bees buzzing about the roses, Avice said, "The fever left you weakened. Stay at Clearwater as long as you need to rest."

From the carriage window, Avice watched the green fields. Peasants worked in them—harvest approached—but every now and then, one would point out the carriage, and they would all look. Every time, Avice looked at her hands. She had not done so ill by her lands.

The carriage crossed a bridge, and the manor house came into sight. About it, roses bloomed profusely: red, pink, and yellow. Even the grass, growing greenly, showed no sign of where the curse had struck.

The carriage stopped. Avice descended and drew a deep breath. She had seen the wizard from that window, and so he had to have stood there, and that grass was the new growth after the curse broke—

The door opened, and the roses nodded in the breeze from the motion. Justin stood in the doorway. He did not step toward her—only smiled.

"The king," said Avice, "was pleased with your efforts on my behalf. Less pleased that you were not there to hear his praises."

Justin raised an eyebrow. "And you? Are you pleased with my efforts on your behalf?"

"Quite," she said, and smiled.

The Emperor's Clothes

The court's finery gleamed before the dock, the officials standing in full robes in scarlet and orange, the servants moving sprightly in gold and black livery, the courtiers crowding about in rose-red and blue and green, bedecked with gold and silver. Matthaios sat back in the barge, hung in peacock blue, as the swans serenely drew it up to the dock. They must think the proposed match important. A marriage between the Emperor Basil and the Princess Zoe might ameliorate the hostility between the lands, but this court was bedecked as for a coronation.

The barge reached the deck, and whatever unseen sorcerer guided it, it slid into place without so much as a quiver. Matthaios rose to his feet. He had done himself up in brocade, as well as the boat, but then, he was the ambassador to discuss the match. The king and the princess had had his garments embroidered in gold and bedecked with opals.

At the dock, a scarlet-clad official bowed deeply to greet him. He wore a golden chain of office about his neck—a chamberlain's badge. Matthaios bowed, not so deeply. The chamberlain escorted him up the first flight of stairs. At the castle door, the emperor Basil descended, to show his respect for a foreign king's ambassador, and in the sunlight, his crown glinted. His robes of cloth-of-gold glittered, showing lions and sunbursts woven into the cloth, and set with the finest of rubies. All about, courtiers bowed and curtseyed, and kept still, their heads bent.

The silence was so profound that the hoarse voice carried over the crowd: "The Emperor has no clothes on!"

Matthaios blinked and looked at the emperor. Basil still wore his golden robes—and now, a thunderous expression as well.

Soldiers converged on the man, in the back of the crowd, where the people had pulled back from a haggard man, ragged in gray, his hair ash white. As if he did not notice the soldiers, he bellowed on. "The Emperor has no clothes on!"

Matthaios glanced at the chamberlain, who looked distressed. "I have heard the tales," he observed.

"It was *years* ago. It wasn't even His Imperial Majesty," said the chamberlain. "It was his great uncle. An old man at the time."

An old man who had been renowned for his sagacity, before he lost his wits, thought Matthaios. "And the one who proclaimed it was a child."

The chamberlain shuddered, and words seemed to flow from his mouth. "A child *then*, but he was so taken by the notion that he alone—that no one had seen it—that he proclaims it again and again, until the emperor humanely had him detained, and still whenever he escapes, and prides himself on his superior vision. . . ." The chamberlain collected himself. "Very shocking that it should happen now, but you need not fear that he will distress the Princess Zoe. He escapes his keepers not twice in a decade."

The guards, their shoulders set, dragged the man off. "Lord Matthaios, do not let them deceive you! Do not profess it because they all say so! Do not *believe* it because they all say so!" The first guard yanked open a gate, and the others dragged him through. "Warn the princess!"

Matthaios turned his attention back to the stairs that the emperor climbed down. Matthaios reminded himself of his king's dignity and honor. He straightened and watched the emperor's descent as the man continued to scream, the sound only muffled by the wall. He did not flinch when a door cracked shut, and the screams were cut off. The emperor managed to walk with dignity. The stiff robes aided there. They also, noted Matthaios, made him look older than his age.

The emperor reached Matthaios. Matthaios bowed. The formal courtesies were exchanged.

The emperor inclined his head. "I regret the discourtesy to which you were exposed."

Matthaios considered Princess Zoe, and the court that she lived in, where cutting out such a lunatic's tongue would be regarded as foolish clemency, when the knave could just be strangled. He bowed again. "The Princess Zoe will be much taken by this demonstration of your magnanimity and forbearance toward a poor lunatic."

The emperor straightened a little and noticeably brightened, seeming much nearer his actual age. The murmurs from the courtiers sounded approving. Matthaios wondered what the lunatic would think of such a flattering description, and then smiled a little. He doubted that, if he heard it, he would ever realize it was quite true.

Mermaids' Song

Sunlight slanted between two of the port's ramshackle buildings. In a tavern, the drinkers already grew rowdy, singing some ballad off-key.

He should not have haggled so long over the bread, Nicolas thought, hurrying along, but money grew short, and the chapel could never count on more. He came around a corner and wrinkled his nose at the harbor's stench. At least he was no longer the little boy that the other children could rob so easily.

"Shoulda, shoulda. . . ." A whore leaned against a wooden doorframe. She waved her wine cup in the air. Nicolas pulled back. In the port, there was no telling when violence would erupt. He could remember that this one was Petronella, but not whether she was prone to fights.

On the other hand, pirates and whores were also prone to penitence when maudlin drunk, which kept him and Father Phillip from starvation. He did not run.

"You're Nic-o-las. Father Phillip's altar boy. The boy that that Berengeria gave to the Church." Petronella hiccupped. "And the Church gave back to us—to that chapel. Damn chapel." She shook her head. "Should never have gone. . . wouldna have heard 'em if I. . . ." When her voice trailed off, she stood as stiffly as the statues out in the chapel of Stella Maris. Nicolas's tongue touched his lip. He wondered if she would speak again.

"Heard mermaids singing."

Nicolas looked warily at her. The mermaids had returned, he had seen one that morning, and Father Phillip had grumbled, but how could that have inspired this—fit?

Petronella's hand went to her pocket. "Hold your hands, Nic-o-las."

Metal glinted in her hands. Nicolas held out his, and coins clattered in his fingers. His eyes widened. Some were silver, and one shone gold.

"Too late—pray for me, Nic-o-las. . . ." Petronella reeled against the door. "Your Star of the Sea—she can guide. . . ."

Petronella looked younger than many whores on the docks—she still had some looks. Nicolas looked quickly away, his face heating. In some ways, venturing into port, where the whores plied their trade, had been easier when he was younger. But, he had his duty. He put the coins away, hoping no one else had seen them. Petronella did not look ill, but she seemed remorseful enough. "Mistress Petronella, you should confess."

"No time, no time. . . ." Tears rolled down her face. Nicolas gulped.

He clutched the pouch of coins as he hurried down the streets. The evening cast even longer shadows, now. When a priest could not be obtained, confession could be made to a layman, and he had persuaded her, despite her ramblings about mermaids, and knowing that the drink was the bulk of her remorse. His fingers traced the gold. She would have drunk the money, he told himself, but she might not remember in the morning. More than one penitent had shown up at the chapel, sober. Nicolas had learned the hard way not to spend the money, or even tell Father Phillip of it, until a few days had passed.

Someone came after him. Nicolas gave a wary glance at the shadows on the wall ahead of him and darted down the alleyway, past the buildings and out onto the rocks. The chapel sat ahead of him, on the promontory.

In spite of himself, he glanced back. The threesome stood in the building and watched him. A breeze carried the smell of dead fish and a few words: "Saw mermaids. Don't want. . . ."

Nicolas walked on. A sailor's superstition, that hearing the mermaids' song meant death—of a piece with their belief that it was unlucky to let a priest, or even an altar boy, onboard ship. That the mermaids often came to that stretch of shore meant that the port had not yet engulfed the chapel, but sailors' superstitions were as unfit for an altar boy as for a priest. Father Dominic's querulous voice echoed in his memory: "A misapprehension arising from confusion with the *siren*, which dwells in more southerly waters, and can lure sailors to their deaths."

He had been easy to impress, when he was eight, Nicolas thought. He clambered over the rocks and turned his thoughts to Petronella's offering. This many coins he had to hide, or Father Phillip send the bishop's share at once, and the bishop would wonder what they concealed, that they did not pay this much every month.

Nicolas leapt on a ridge of rock and walked along it, with a stretch of rocky beach descending to the ebb tide below him. The clean scent of the sea came in a breeze. "'Behold I am sending you as sheep among wolves. Be therefore as wise as serpents and as innocent as doves.'" At the ridge's end, he leapt down again. Father Phillip had the doves' innocence; Nicolas had to have the serpents' wisdom.

Besides, other churches had poor boxes, and that money never made it to Stella Maris, though their quarter was the poorest.

The sound of the ebb tide's waves was steady, with gulls' cries, and something else. Nicolas paused, scowling. Music came from the waters, voices singing on the wind. Sunlight glinted orange from the waves, and its slantwise rays sketched out every ripple. Every now and then, one rose from the water: a sleek body with pale smooth skin from the waist up and glittering scales below.

Nicolas glanced about. In the shadows at the shoreline, most of the mermaids perched on the rocks and seaweed, visible now that he knew where to look.

And singing.

One glanced at him, smiled, and turned to a companion. Briefly, song gave way to giggles.

Nicolas swallowed. The song, taken up again, pursued him. I have to hurry because Father Phillip may not be well enough to ring the Angelus, he told himself.

He scrapped his hands on rough stones, climbing, and drew blood. The salt from the stones stung in the wounds. He barely noticed and did not slow. His breath was harsh from his speed, but he could hear the mermaids' song above it.

He forced himself to draw a deep breath before he rushed on. That was a sailors' superstition.

He climbed off the rocks to the sand and grass at the end of the promontory, and glanced back. Half a dozen mermaids glanced slyly at him. He shuddered and walked as fast as the sandy footing would let him. The Angelus bell hung in its little tower, by the chapel, among the roses. He wavered. The mermaids were like the Fair Folk, and the Fair Folk feared church bells.

Before he could think further, he strode to the Angelus bell and rang it. The clear golden note echoed over the grass and water. Nicolas closed his eyes and prayed silently, The angel of God declared unto Mary....

Father Phillip emerged from the chapel. "What are you doing, Nicolas? It is not time for the Angelus."

Nicolas opened his mouth, envisioned the lecture on sailors' superstitions, and said, instead, "Didn't think. Was worried about being late."

Father Phillip rolled his eyes. "Come in for the evening service."

Nicolas followed. The wild pink roses, with only five petals but the size of his hand, filled the air with sweetness, and he drew in a deep breath.

Predictably enough, no one came out to the chapel for the service—had it not been raised by a king in thanksgiving for delivery from a sea storm, the chapel of Stella Maris would long ago have vanished—but Father Phillip paid the lack of congregation no heed, and Nicolas, being used to it, served.

"Those that go down to the sea in ships, trading in the great waters, see the works of the Lord, His wonders in the deep. . . . They cried to the Lord in the distress, and He rescued them from their troubles."

Nicolas stared fixedly at the Psalm. He was not in distress. The mermaids' song was not dangerous. And he should assist at the service, not brood over the mermaids.

When they came to the chapel door again, the sunset was in full color. Father Phillip drew in a deep breath. "Those roses went well." He shook his head. "Almost wish that I had not started that Mary Garden, but the roses did survive."

He maundered on, on the significance of roses. Nicolas, having heard about the Rose of Sharon before, looked out to sea. The colors on the waters almost hid them, but the mermaids rose and sank in the waves. Then two swam up to lie on their bellies on the sand and glance at him, and giggled to each other.

"'In the midst of life, we are in the midst of death,'" said Father Phillip from the doorway. By the hearth, Nicolas looked up from the porridge. Gray morning light shone in, and the dew-laden air overlaid the smell of smoke and porridge, but he could not see whom Father Phillip talked so solemnly with. He stirred the porridge again. A log fell, stirring up ash.

The shutting of the door dimmed the room. "A sad thing," said Father Phillip, returning to the fireplace. The orange light brought out the wrinkles in his face. "Lysette insisted that Petronella confessed herself before she died."

"Petronella!?" Nicolas's voice cracked. That was chance, he thought, his heart hammering. The mermaids' song was superstition. Father Phillip looked at him, and he had to rally his thoughts, or the priest would question him without end. "That was why I was late, Father. She thought she would die, and gave me money." He glanced at the porridge. No large bubbles pushed through the beige surface, and he could leave it a moment without its burning. He scrambled off to get the coins. Not all, he reminded himself, but he would have to give Father Phillip the gold coin, for it could not be split up. He swallowed. The woman who had given him them was dead, just as she had been certain.

Aren't you glad to persuade her to confess? said one priggish thought, but the thought was unable to shake his horror. He fought to concentrate on the money.

The priest looked at him all the time he scrambled for the coins. "I had forgotten in the jumble of putting the food all away. But since she said she was dying, I told her she should confess. She didn't think she could make it here. . . ."

"I confess," said Father Phillip, "that I have doubted whether you ever listened to your lessons."

Nicolas felt his face heat. Father Phillip was sometimes more astute than he appeared.

"But that makes it clear. She may receive Christian burial." He looked at Nicolas. "Remember her in your prayers."

Nicolas bobbed his head, but the memory that clung to him was the mermaids' song he had heard. He shivered. He would pray for protection, as well.

A plopping sound came from the porridge, as an enormous bubble burst, forming a ripple on the surface. Nicolas leapt to it, before it burned. He could not let such folly distract him.

"You!"

The oak of a man, looming over everyone else in the street, looked straight at Nicolas. Nicolas's mouth went dry. An enormous, florid man—from his clothing, one of the pirates that the king's officials winked at. Nicolas ransacked his memory for his name. Maximinus, the pirate called himself, a name no more his own than the names that the whores gave.

"You were the boy at the grave—you belong to the chapel." Maximinus stepped forward. Less drunk than Petronella, Nicolas thought. He glanced about for a getaway. Sailors were worse than whores when drunk, and pirates were the worst of the sailors.

Maximinus's voice boomed again, drawing attention all around. "I heard mermaids!"

It was chance, Nicolas thought, but he could not get the words to his numb mouth.

A pouch—a large pouch—clinked as Maximinus held it out. Reluctantly, Nicolas took it. It felt heavy for its size.

"My end's a-coming, boy!" His voice lowered to a stentorian whisper. "Pray for me."

Nicolas bobbed his head and wondered if he should try to persuade Maximinus to confess. The pirate leaned against the wall, maundering on, unintelligibly. Nicolas, feeling cold and reluctant, clenched the purse. He had persuaded Petronella.

Maximinus groaned. The sound turned Nicolas's chill to ice. The pirate pulled away from the wall and toppled. A woman's shrill scream rose behind him. Nicolas leapt away, but

Maximinus's outstretched hand still brushed his feet. His face was contorted.

"Good God!" Someone leapt out of the tavern. Moments later, Nicolas pulled back from the forming crowd. Exclamations dinned in Nicolas's ears, until one settled in his thoughts: "The priest must be told!"

"I'll tell Father Phillip," said Nicolas, and sprinted down the street, towards Stella Maris. The pouch felt heavier than it had when Maximinus gave him it. More gold perhaps—and some of it was oddly shaped and too lumpy to be coins. It might be jewelry.

It wouldn't matter to him, only to Father Phillip, he realized as he came out on the rocks. With the high tide, the mermaids disported on the rocks near the path, but they posed no danger to him. He had already heard the mermaids singing.

Even if that were not a sailors' superstition.

"There he is!" The words echoed like the Angelus bell: a sweet woman's voice. In spite of himself, Nicolas turned. A mermaid smiled at him. Her eyes and hair were as brown as seaweed, but her skin was pearly white. Nicolas gulped and kept his gaze carefully above her shoulders.

The mermaid laughed. "Silly boy," she said fondly. "We do not wish to drown you. We wish only to claim our own." Her gaze went to the pouch. "Pearls are sea, and belong to us."

"Pearls?" Nicolas looked at the pouch. He had not even looked inside. "You claim all pearls?"

Another mermaid, her hair as red as coral, smiled from the next rock. "How else could we know that you carry pearls, when we have not seen inside?" Her smile deepened, and her tail flipped up, the ruddy scales gleaming in the sunlight. "Open it and see."

They looked smug and as if concealing something. But—did they really know what Maximinus had given him?

Almost without his willing it, Nicolas's fingers went to the pouch lacing. The mermaids watched, their murmurs not rising over the sound of the waves enough to be heard. The pouch slid open, and a string of pearls lay on the top. Nicolas lifted it. These pearls could pay the parish's charity for years: the sick, the orphans needing care, the widows without support, the boys who needed apprenticeships, the girls without dowries, the poor women who needed midwives.

"Our pearls," said the mermaid. She extended a hand.

Nicolas's hand tightened about the string. "Why do you want it?" His voice sounded thick.

"That which belongs to the sea," said the mermaid, amused, "belongs to the sea." She glanced at him through her eyelashes. "What do it matter, *why*?"

He tried to think, to remember, and then he recalled a shipwreck. He raised his head. "A ship went down—down the shore a few years ago." The mermaid lowered her hand, seeming to accept the diversion for a moment. "Since the pearls are yours, because they are sea, the rubies on it must be mine, because they are land."

For a moment, nothing moved but the pounding of waves. Then the mermaid pouted and slipped back into the sea, with a faint splash. Nicolas stuffed the pearls back into the pouch— deep into it, where they could not just fall out—and spotted the bracelets of jade, the necklace of emeralds, the. . . he yanked it shut and scrambled away.

Why did they want the pearls? he wondered as he climbed a rock. Father Dominic's voice came back to him, dryly warning that all sea creatures took part in the mutability of water, and were prone to whims.

And Father Phillip would declare that seeking an explanation of why a woman wanted jewels was folly.

The waves rose higher than before, he noticed suddenly. It was a spring tide, to be sure, but the waves reached past the high tide mark, with no storm wind to stir them up. Mermaid heads bobbed in the rising waves, streaming water from their hair, and the rocks shifted underfoot, far more than they ever had before.

Undermining?! went a frantic thought, but Nicolas's feet took off without paying heed, or questioning how the waves could work so quickly. He scrambled up on the higher ground. The pouch lurched, and something went flying. He glanced back in time to see the emeralds landing among the rocks. I should have retied the laces, no matter how much I wished to be gone, he realized with a sickening dread.

The leading mermaid rose up out of the waters. "It's not the pearls, but it will do. Come help me move the rocks."

Nicolas saw the emeralds glitter in the crevice. He would have to move stones to get at it, but the mermaids, with their tails, would have more difficulty shifting them than he would. He looked about and laid the pouch high, where the sand first touched the stone, before clambering back.

The mermaid glowered at him. "Why do you have to it *all*? You won't even wear them. . . ."

I doubt you will put them to good works, thought Nicolas. The stones were rough under his hands, he garnered more than one scrape, but the emeralds came free.

A mermaid clapped her hands in glee. Nicolas looked up. An august mermaid, her black hair sweeping back from her face, swam toward the shore. She held in her hands an enormous pearl, gleaming white. Nicolas shoved a rock on top of another, and stopped, watching her and holding the stone in place.

"The Pearl of Truth! Look, oh land-dweller." She looked down at the pearl. "I am a mermaid. He is a land-dweller. The necklace he drew out first was pearls."

A rock slid from Nicolas's hand as he wondered, and bashed his forearm. He scowled.

The mermaid smiled. "This that I hold is an emerald."

The pearl went black as a night with the sky muffled in storm clouds.

"The necklace he is trying to retrieve is also pearls. He is a merman, and I am a land woman." The pearl remained ceaselessly black. The mermaid drew a deep breath and glanced through her eyelashes at Nicolas. "Whoever hears the song of the mermaid will die."

The pearl turned white again, all but glowing in her hands.

After a moment of deafening silence, Nicolas heard his pulse hammering in his ears. The emeralds glinted. His hand wavered on the stone. He could let it go, leave the emeralds out of reach, and flee. He would die, and not need it, and Father Phillip was likely to let it go into the hands of the bishops and do no good for the poor.

The mermaid smiled.

Nicolas set his mouth. Was likely to—not, was certain to. Being about to die was no time to fall into sin. Petronella had that right, and he would not fall below her level. He hefted up the stone and, after a moment's thought, hurled it over the others, into the sea. The mermaids jerked back, and it landed with a splash. Nicolas yanked back the last stone and grabbed the emeralds. Even as he straightened, he heard the mermaids singing again.

Father Phillip had taken Maximinus's charity as a token of good faith, and so Nicolas stood in the tiny graveyard as the internment ended. All the mourners who had come to stare started to babble, of this, that, and the mermaids' song.

"He was doomed, he heard mermaids singing." One haggish woman shook her head.

Nicolas hesitated. It was a sailors' superstition. Perhaps the sailors knew more about it. "How soon?" She blinked and looked at him with rheumy eyes. "How soon after you hear mermaids singing do you die?"

"Within a day, my boy, within a day."

"Not hardly." A fishwife put her burly hands on her hips. "Maximinus heard them last week—he griped 'fore Petronella died."

"They're sea creatures," said a sailor, wearing an exotic scarf from a southern port. "They go by the moon, like the tides—the song'll kill you in a month."

Clamor broke out around him. Everyone in the port, it seemed, had a time, and no more than six or seven were adduced. Nicolas tried to escape, and a whore drew him out. She nodded to him and winked. "It's a year and a day. Old Jake heard the mermaids and lived out the year and a day. You can die any time in there, but you can live as long as a year and a day."

Then, though Nicolas, feeling chilled, he had best prepare for it to happen that night, if death could come at any time. He remembered the mermaid's smile. She was trying to frighten you into leaving the emeralds, he told himself. You heard the singing the day before.

"Old Jake!" Another woman slapped her arm. "Old Jake dreamed of hearing mermaids, there was no way he could have lived that long after it!"

"Such a long face," said Father Phillip, as they walked through the grass. "I did not think you so fond of Maximinus."

Nicolas drew a deep breath. The grass flavored the sea smell on the breeze. "Father, will you hear my confession?"

"Very good, my boy. It is always wise to remember these things, even when you are young." He looked ahead. "As soon as we reached the chapel."

Nicolas nodded but glanced sideways. Mermaids played in the waves. One raised her head and shoulder above the waves and waved at him.

"I will rejoice when they leave," Father Phillip said. "The superstitious sailors afraid to come to services because of the song—as if they came eagerly when the mermaids are elsewhere!"

They had the pearl, thought Nicolas. It told the truth. I am going to die. The thought merged with the sound of the lapping waves. I am going to die.

And then another thought struck him.

"Oh, mermaids!" he caroled, standing on the rocks. The mermaids, out in the surf, seemed at first not to hear him, and then to be discussing whether to come in. Nicolas smiled. They would come if he waited long enough—he had survived making his confession, he would survive here, as well. And then, half a dozen of them did, and the first was the one who had asked for the pearls.

"Oh land-dweller! Have you come to bring us our pearls?"

Nicolas shrugged. "Perhaps you could fetch me the Pearl of Truth and answer me a question."

The mermaid's smile vanished. "Perhaps." Her bell-like voice was cool. "But why would we?"

"You told me I would die." The mermaid looked smug. That had not been what she feared he would ask. Nicolas pressed on. "You did not tell me how soon." The smugness slipped again. "And it is the lot of men to die, sooner or later, whether they hear you or not."

Her face filled with fury. No need for the Pearl of Truth now, Nicolas thought, and laughed. The offended mermaids dived off, all about him.

You could still die tomorrow, said a cold thought. They were right in that much. His laughter subsided, and he looked out over the waves. No mermaid heads emerged as the waves lapped at the shore.

Then, that had always been true. He would have to learn to live with the knowledge. Nicolas managed a smile. "Oh, mermaids, you should not leave. Father Phillip would want to thank you, for persuading me to think seriously of death."

A mermaid emerged, to give him a look so indignant that he laughed again.

Witch-Prince Ways

Katie Green, bright as a dream, hid in the hills, not fit to be seen.

Still sore, her bundle in her arms, she hurried down the muddy road, over leaves sodden from snowmelt and spring rain. It's not safe, it's not safe, thrummed in her thoughts. Peering about at the crossroads, she ran her tongue over her dry lips, and her heart hammered. Even had Jack lived, they—her kin or his—would kill a baby. (What were life and love and kinship when revenge could be won?) Over winter, she had seen naught and heard naught—they had no taste for roving through frost and snow and brooks heavy with ice, belike—but spring came. Earliest spring, with only the boldest sprouts unfurling, with only bits of buds on the most sheltered trees, but already kin of hers, sneaking about hillsides, asked of her swelling with child, of Jack, found in the winter wood, and buried in the old graveyard in stone-hard ground. (How the grave-digger had grumbled!)

She bit her lip. Had he borne any wound at all, as much as a bruise, she would have known it to be murder, but he had just lain, cold and pale, on wet dark leaf mould with leafless trees all about.

The old oak, towering at the crossroads, was bare as a gallows tree, but under it, scattered snowdrops flowered whitely. Katie pulled her bundle closer. A chance, her only chance—his only chance—she glanced down. Solemn, the baby looked back with eyes as dark as Jack's. Her teeth tightened on her lip. Spring meant spring travelers. Who might—not being of her kin, or Jack's—take up a baby.

Wrapping the blankets more tightly, and laying the oiled sealskin under him against the wet, Katie left him among the snowdrops. She put the little saint's medal in the bundle, hoping travelers would guess to call him Kit, christened Christopher for the saint whose chapel lay by their cottage—for who else? for any in their kin? whether hers or Jack's?—hoping St. Christopher would watch his wandering little namesake when his mother could not.

She hurried off, pulling her shawl close about his head for fear he—always a sweet baby—would chose this time to wail, just as she deserved it. . . .

Wind tossed the branches and sent splatters of rainwater, cold as snow, down on her. Katie stopped. For a breath, in water-clear clarity, she thought. As clear as some girl who picked a four-leafed clover and saw through some spell. Water trickled down her face, and she did not raise a hand against it, too deep to even think of it. She had nowhere to go. Not hereabouts. Jack's widow was welcome in neither his kin's house, nor her own's.

For a moment, she breathed air smelling of rain-wet earth and moldering old leaves. She, she, she—could be a spring traveler and take her son. She ran, mud clinging to her steps and slowing her.

At the oak, her baby was nowhere to be seen. The only trace was her own footsteps, welling with water, and the press on the earth where she had laid him down. No one had left any mark when Kit had been taken up again. Not a footprint, not a bent leaf—

The medal lay there, too.

Her tongue felt like lead in her mouth. Who—who—who—went her thoughts like an owl—as if any but the Witch Prince could snatch Kit away with not a mark of his feet.

And he had hunted the night of Jack's dying, she *knew* that, old men and little children had muttered it, and she had never so much as thought of how Jack had come to lie among leafless trees and dead leaves. . . she forced her breath in and out, and the air hurt. The Witch Prince had witched her wits away. Her hand formed a fist. But he'd let her wits escape like a rabbit, and now they would run, uphill and down, and through all the woods and over every brook.

"Oh no oh no." The witching woman, wrapped in brown, rocked back and forth on her stool. Her candle, in its candlestick, sat on the hearth beside her, and the flaxen flame wavered from the wind of her passing. Candlelight danced, casting shifting shadows over her lined face, and vast shadows over the wall.

(No place for Katie to sit but on the cold hearth. About, dried herbs and their shadows loomed like skeletons.)

Katie's tongue touched her lips.

"Oh no oh no the witch prince has his ways and has your babe." She chortled, leaning forward. "Muddled your wits so you left your babe—you fight him now? Where he lives? You do not know his ways, you do not. He hunts deer, he hunts hounds, he hunts men, he hunts the wind, he hunts the moon—"

"I must." Katie's breath came light and fast.

The witching woman grinned. Her few teeth were like moon-lit scraps of cloud. "When you found your man, your husband dear, lying in the woods after *his* hunting? You *must*?"

Katie swallowed, too frightened to tell which affrighted her worse: the witch's knowing that Katie and Jack had wed in the wood, with naught but the words of marriage, not one witness to them, or her knowing that the Witch-Prince's hunt had struck Jack down.

"He'd've left a stock to fool you, to look like your Kit, if he had aught to fear from you—"

Her breasts ached with the need for nursing. "I must, I must—I go to Rook's Wood whatever you do, whatever you say, I know as well as you where the Witch-Prince lives—"

The witching woman cackled—long and long, stopping only when she was breathless and shaking her head. "You will, you will—that's why you sit here when you could be doing what you say you do—"

Katie dragged in her breath and straightened. "Tell me that you can do naught to help me, and I'll go."

The witching woman, frozen like an icicle in the dead of winter, eyed her. Candlelight glittered from her unmoving eye, with the candle flame standing as still as a mountain.

Katie clamped her mouth shut, almost did not breathe. Every tale said the witching woman could trick, could mislead, could leave out, but could not lie. She could hold her tongue to find if it were true.

The witching woman snorted. "There's a charm for the castle." She looked aside, as if to talk to the candle flame. "She'll be wiser ere she's much older, if she uses that."

"Always better, being wiser," said Katie.

The witching woman chortled, and the candle flame quivered. "Wise against wiser—she's not wise enough for that."

Katie folded her arms. "Too much a fool to leave without the charm."

"She'll be wet and cold ere she's much older," said the witching woman to the candle flame. "Ere she's wiser."

She should've left it to full day. Noontide, at least. After that hour, better. Even early in spring, the sun brought the warmth.

Still, with chilly mist curling about pale birches and leafless brush, she plodded up the hillside, by the brook as it babbled and murmured over rounded gray stone. Ice gathered only here and there, swan-white lacing caught in niches of stones, but the waters would be snowmelt cold. With no path to lead her, she could not wander far from the waters. She clambered on. Her ankle turned sometimes on the jumble of stone, and her fingers tried to bite into rough stone to steady her.

The hillside rose higher, and flattened. Bits of blue stood between the trees ahead, and the stream widened before her. The current slowed, too, to amble along the streambed. That was well, since in the waters spread an island, scarcely large as a cottage. Three slim birches, their trunks snowy pale, grew there, perched in the jumble of stones.

Katie looked at the waters. Too deep to wade. She bit her lip. And soaked clothing would not keep her warm.

Grimacing, she turned aside. She should have waited, she told herself again, while she stripped off her clothing and draped it over the nearest brush—not heaping it on the ground, the only shield she could make against the cold. The cloth hung there, as dark as a crow's wing or the damp bark about her, like dead leaves that the winter had not managed to tear from the tree.

She ran into the waters before she could think.

The waters were so cold they burned. Gasping, she splashed through, though the water rose to her waist, and out to the island where she shivered more than any leaf in any wind—the charm, the charm, she scrambled over to the first birch and checked its roots. The rocks trembled from her shaking, and she bashed her fingers, ice-white with cold, on the stone, but she found no charm. She scrambled to the next, where the roots held it no more than the last. And to the third, eying each root with care— she would freeze, she did not have the time to search for it—

A dark ring, made of nails, lay about one white root. Her hands plunged for it. A breeze made them shake worse than ever; she barely managed to brush the ring with her hand, and the point of a nail drew blood like a tiny red bud. She forced down both hands to seize the ring and wiggle it, bit by bit, off the root.

Her hands trembled, and her clothing lay on the other side. Still she turned her attention to the ring, seizing it in one hand to force it on a finger of another. And when she looked back at her clothing, she said to herself, "Fancy fishing it from the waters?" It did not hearten her as she shivered her way to the shore.

With the ring heavy about her finger, she plunged back in, chilling herself to the bone. She barely scuttled out again. With mist-pale hands she dressed, taking twice and thrice as long to don her clothes, but even with all of them on, she still shivered and trembled.

"Speed," she told herself. "For warmth. And to reach Rook's Wood."

With the ring on her finger and her blood bright red on it like autumn leaves on a dark swelling river, she walked off—better to run, but even walking she was shivering unsteady. Some ways, with roots and bumps, she staggered along. Some hillsides, bearing spreads of stone loose across their slope, she walked round, no matter how her feet ached with walking.

Mist left, and she walked in the valley, before she felt warm again. Clouds lay cold overhead, ready to rain. She walked on, charm held tight in her hand.

Rain splattered on boughs overhead and laid splotches on the ground. She lifted her hood to shelter her head and walked on.

Rook's Wood was thorn in the rain, the bare boughs as black as the parliament of rooks that clamored from the branches, and the thorns looked sharper than the nails of the ring. With her hood up, Katie saw not a sign of aught that was strange.

Her thumb brushed her ring. Good for getting near, but once near, she needed to see. She lowered her hood again. The misty rain brushed her with cold and damp as she walked among the thorns and wondered whether she could search it out, when the witching woman said naught of whether the charm might find his hall.

Then they wandered, in and out, through the thorns.

But for black eyes, beady, bird-like, she might have missed them. Things like gnarled roots, clad in gray and brown like long-moldering leaves, they scampered, not straight, but bent like birds hurtling through leaves. And she saw their bright eyes, gleaming in stray light, but they did not see her.

In, out, went her breath. Near, she had to be near for those to scurry so freely. She saw naught else new, naught but thorn and dead leaves. She stole on, soft as she could, with leaves yielding underfoot. They scuttled about her, their heads bent, on furtive tasks. Some lugged enormous sacks, of black burlap, twice or thrice their size, with lumps in them so odd she could not guess at the contents. All glanced about, as if fearing the pounce of a cat, or that a knight would stop them in their ways.

Katie walked on, and on, over hillocks, into hollows—evading some of those for the black mud, or even pooled water—and they still swarmed about her, and her heart sank. How far did they fare, through the Rook's Woods? Were they any sign of that the Witch Prince was here?

With the way he hunted, he might range far indeed, leaving these petty creatures. . . .

Her mouth twisted. She touched the charm with her thumb. The nail's point pricked but drew no blood. Should she forsake her child and join the spring travelers already? After she had gone to fetch the ring? She walked on, over a higher hill, where she looked down in a valley.

A castle of thorn and stone, black with the spring rains, as black as the wood's rooks—the valley was deep, but the castle reared up as high as the hills about it. Gates towered, black as a starless night.

Katie walked before those gates and stood, peering up at them. No wind stirred her skirt or tugged at her hair. The ring had got her here. It would not let her speak to him, or even get her within.

She nearly closed her hand in a fist about it. She thought of wandering about the castle like a wild thing, but the thorns were sharp. Perhaps a mouse could steal through them. She was not a mouse.

Slowly, she took the ring off.

After a minute, the gates creaked open, like the boughs of mighty trees in a high wind. Perhaps eyes, dark as a well, peered at her from odd corners; perhaps not. The air did not stir. When the gates stopped, it seemed as if they had hung open for years; they offered no welcome.

Clutching the ring in her hand, Katie walked in.

The castle looked like a forest inside, with trees, and roots, and outcroppings of rock among dead leaves that had moldered into drabness. But here, all about, the Witch-Prince's court spread, those things like gnarled roots in little man-shapes. Even at court, they wore gray and brown like dead leaves. She scarce could tell them from the forest floor where they sat on roots and outcroppings of rock.

In the center, the Witch-Prince himself loomed, as drably dressed as his court, wearing a crown like braided branches. At his feet, her little son, as white as the snowdrops, cooed, out of her reach.

"Kit," she said, but the words would not leave her lips.

The Witch-Prince turned his eyes, as dark as a bear's, on her. All about, the root men whispered, and stared, and hid their gnarled little faces behind their hands to chortle.

"Heh," said the Witch-Prince. "Came all this way and has naught to ask for."

"Give him back to me!" she called. "Give him back!" She took a step forward and could not take another. She did not know what kept her back, whether mud clinging to her feet, or air thickening before her until she could not push through it.

"He is *my* son!" The words tore out, pleading, demanding, begging, without interruption until her throat was hoarse with speaking. . . .

"Please," she said again, roughly, afraid she could push no more words out. The cold air did naught to soothe how it burned.

The court abandoned all pretense of courtesy to laugh and laugh and laugh. They fell from their roots and rocks and rolled through mud and leaves, chortling and kicking the air.

"Not even fit for a nurse," rumbled the Witch-Prince. "So silly as to tell all!"

"You have no title to him," said Katie, forcing words through her painful throat.

The Witch-Prince sat back. Kit cooed, and her heart hammered. He could not fathom that his mother pleaded for him.

"You put it aside and so had no more need for it." The Witch-Prince nodded, solemnly. He gestured upward. "I have the crown, I am the king, I rule on such cases—"

The root-men chorused their assent, their twig-like heads bobbing. The crown gave him the rule.

"You had no more need for it."

Though her throat burned, she opened her mouth again.

Wind erupted from nowhere and buffeted her with blows. Katie staggered back. The court roared with laughter again and pointed twig-like fingers. She staggered on and on, out. The wind sometimes shoved with no step on her part and sometimes hurled her into mud and dead leaves, and did not stop with the gates closing behind her.

Outside the castle—nearly outside Rook's Wood—the wind forced her through an icy stream and dumped her, her skirts dripping, on the other bank. She sat on dead, damp leaves in utterly still air and stared at her hand, still clutching the ring, but numb and white from chill. She stared at it for a long time. Her throat burned as if she had eaten red-hot coals.

She still had nowhere to go. She staggered to her feet.

O Kit my child, she thought. The ring went back on her finger.

She had to wait. And wait. Little courtiers skittered about the castle like wind-blown leaves, and whispered and chortled to each other. Wind blew by. Rain skittered through the barren branches, making her pull her cloak more tightly about her head, till it shadowed her face.

When the gate first opened, she bit her lip. It opened no more than to let a root man out. Even were she standing by it, she could never get in before it closed.

She drew closer. Did the thorn grow as thick as about a sleeping princess's castle? Could she steal within?

A swarm of the root men, squabbling, drew near, and the gate started to open. Katie caught up an acorn and hurled it among them, hitting one. A shrill accusation followed, and Katie scurried, having no notion how long the quarrel, and blows, would last. She did not glance back within the gate.

With the ring, skulking around the castle did not draw their eye. No one marked the slight little haunt the castle had gained. Root-men courtiers played dice with acorns. Tiny cooks lugged out a coppery pot that could have held twenty of them, and fed her son from it. Her mouth tightened.

She did not stop watching. Not when they chortled and danced about with Kit, jeering of their cunning in claiming him. Not when the Witch-Prince took her son up in his arms as if he had claim to him in truth. Not when Kit, squealing with glee, batted at the crown. . . .

Katie froze. The baby batted again and again. Slowly, she started to creep, reminding herself that the Witch-Prince could put the baby down.

But when her son, gurgling, reached again, the Witch-Prince took off his crown and laid it aside to tease the baby.

Katie swallowed while her heart pounded out the moments. She wondered that even the charm kept them from hearing her heart. She crept again, around and about the courtiers intent on the king and child, until her hands closed about the branches; then fast as a hawk's strike, she snatched the crown to herself.

The branches tangled with her fingers and prodded her arms. Clinging to it, she sat on the cold, damp ground and stared at the Witch-Prince. Kit squealed, holding the eyes of all the court.

Katie drew off the ring, fumbling a little to keep from even letting the crown slip while she did.

A courtier cried out. Grumbling, other root men turned. They fell silent. Before a minute had passed, all the court stared. The courtiers' eyes grew as large as the Witch-Prince's had been, and as for the Witch-Prince's, she had seen smaller millstones.

In a voice as thin as the smallest of breezes, she said, "You put it aside and so had no more need for it."

Her gaze went to her son and back to the Witch-Prince. Wise, the witching woman was; she was now wiser in the Witch-Prince's ways without being much older.

"A trade then," said the Witch-Prince, his voice soft, scare louder than hers.

Katie rocked back and forth. The branches shifted and poked. A trade. Her son for his crown. But after he had the crown back? What would it let him do?

Her mouth tightened in a spasm, and she hefted up the crown. Horror struck his face, making her sure, and she put it on her own head.

As if it shrank in her hands, the branches settled on her head in a perfect fit. Shrieking, "Queen, queen!" the courtiers pressed about her.

Katie rose to her feet. "Give back what was took from me!"

"Queen, queen, queen!" Some swarmed to the Witch-Prince to pry Kit free. He did not fight, but their twig-like fingers had to pry and poke to drag his hands away from the baby. Others scuttled like squirrels in an acorn hunt, for no clear grounds. Deep within the castle, among the thorns, shouts still rose, "Queen, queen!" and she wondered why as the Witch-Prince, dumbstruck, stared into the castle.

Until a throng of the root men tugged forth a man, out from the thorns. A man weary and haggard, his clothing tattered, his eyes bewildered. Then he saw her.

They laid the baby in her arms, and she held him, but her eyes did not turn to Kit, only watched Jack walk toward her, like old tales, of a wooden stock left like a corpse and buried as them while the taken men, or women, or babes, stayed captive. She trembled like a leaf tossed by the wind. She had known, she had remembered for Kit that such things might be done. . . how witched had her wits been?

She lifted her arms. "Your son," she said.

Snowdrops drifted alongside the road, more of them than grew under the oak. Jack and Katie with quick feet picked their way, long past the crossroads where spring travelers passed. The crown sat on her head, like twigs caught in her hair. Kit slept in her arms, wearing the medal for St. Christopher's aid in their travel—Jack told tales of the Witch-Prince and his root men— and Katie asked whether they could pass running water.

A bridge stood ahead.

"No, they can not," said Jack. "They have no way—though with roundabout ways, they can get around."

"Take your son," she said, as they climbed up the bridge, to its height. As Jack cocked an eyebrow and obeyed, her hands went up, to lift up the crown. The tangle rose as one, and caught the sunlight for a moment.

Below, the river rumbled with snow melt.

She threw the crown over. It fell to the river and the snags of wood that caught it and held it there in the flood.

Long hours they had walked, fleeing the Witch-Prince, but Katie fancied she heard a cry of outrage behind her.

Kit squealed, reaching. His father touched his nose, and Kit's hand surged up to swipe Jack's hand.

Katie Green, bright as a dream, lived out her life, despite of their scheme.

Sword and Shadow

Flor combed Sanchia's black hair with unusual jerkiness. "I do not like it, I do not like it one bit, though he's your lord husband. Bringing magic back—too dangerous. Leave it in the mountains. With the shades. . . ."

Sanchia, still despite the tugs on her hair, stared at the distant, purple mountains. Flor presumed on her place and talked nonsense. The shades had slithered from the mountains to kill babes in the cradle and waylay travelers for gold—

"They say your lord won't even tell where he got it!"

The comb hit a tangle, and Flor's voice lowered to mutters as she picked at it.

On the other hand, Flor was not singing praises of the great war, fought in the mountains the last five years, or of the marvelous sword that Lord Alessandro wielded—though its marvels were never the same from one story to the next—and Sanchia had grown weary of that. She breathed deeply. The summer air smelled of horses, of crops in the field, and dust.

I fought a war, she thought. When Sir Adrian defied me, I raised the vassals—those that Alessandro had left me—and forced his obedience, though I was a woman, untrained in war and without magic to aid me. No one sang songs of *me*.

Her mouth twisted. She had to fight not only in her husband's absence, but because of that absence. Had Alessandro held his own lands, Sir Adrian would never have defied *him*.

The comb slid through her hair. "No good will come of this," said Flor. "Returning with a magical sword—how do we know where it came from?"

"I heard you when Rosa was born," Sanchia said. The comb stopped. Sanchia went on. "Angry that my lord was gone, and could not get a son and heir on me. He has returned to the kingdom, and will soon return to my bed."

She would share her bed with a man she had not seen in five years—but Flor nodded. She pulled the comb through last inches of Sanchia's hair, rose, and curtseyed before leaving.

Sanchia breathed out. She was being unjust. Alessandro was as bound to obey the king as Sir Adrian to obey her, and the shades threatened even their lands, if the king did not drive them back. Alessandro had had to leave, and fight.

For five years. Rosa was four, and Alessandro had never seen her. Beatrice, he would not recognize; the daughter who had toddled when he left was now a shy girl.

She slammed her hand against the stones of the wall. Alessandro was her husband, and she would stop this petty resentment of him. Why had she started? She had not seethed, all the years he was gone—only when the news of the war's end, and Alessandro's return, had come.

A clamor sounded below. Servants and men-at-arms surrounded a horseman—a knight, whose tabard bore a coat of arms. Glad of the distraction, Sanchia hurried down, trying to place the gold animal blazoned on green.

She emerged into the courtyard, where half the castle's men and maids had gathered to look. In their middle, the horse still bore the messenger: Sir Marcus, one of Alessandro's men. She could not have placed his coat-of-arms, for he had been knighted in the mountains, and granted it there.

"Lady Sanchia!" The crowds parted, however resentful the maids looked, and Sir Marcus dismounted and swept a bow. "Your lord husband returns, after mighty deeds, winning great fame—and a marvelous sword, if mysterious, as well." He grinned. "He said he will arrive in three days, and you know how he is."

Her fingernails bit her palms again. How could I know? I have not seen him in five years—though he had been punctual before. "We shall receive him gladly."

The servants hurried even before she gave orders—though two whispered that even the men *with* Lord Alessandro did not know where the sword had come from.

Sanchia looked past the walls. The small portion of the road visible to her held no sign of Alessandro's company.

"Which dress, my lady?" said Jeromina.

"The red, I think." Even the red was dark, she thought as Jeromina fetched it, like a sunset on the verge of night. Alessandro would wonder what happened to his jewel-bright bride.

The maid pulled the gown over Sanchia's underdress. The cloth was cool against her bare arms. What had happened was that, in charge of his lands, she had needed the most somber colors she could find, to lend her authority.

"Your jewelry?" said Jeromina. Sanchia considered. She had worn only a piece or two of the loot that Alessandro had sent her over the years, at celebrations, but her husband's arrival was a celebration.

If only of her no longer having to hold his lands for him!

Rosa and Beatrice stood in the antechamber, frightened and brilliant in their finery. Sanchia kissed them both. "How pretty you look. Your father will marvel that his daughters have grown up so charming."

At the mention of Alessandro, Beatrice looked down. Even Rosa seemed subdued. Let him not be late, Sanchia prayed. The children are nervous enough. "Come into the great hall."

She took their hands, and the nurse scurried after. Everyone stood in the hall, making it sibilant with whispers, and wearing their brightest clothing, as if it were Easter. Her dark red would be conspicuous in their midst—as was only fitting for the lady.

Her arrival drew a wave of bows and curtseys, but within moments, their attention returned to the doors.

Sir Marcus stood among the most ornately dressed women. "Yes, the sword is magic, the king had never seen one before, but Lord Alessandro should, of course, hold such a treasure—"

The king, thought Sanchia, could have summoned younger sons, landless ones who needed to make their fortunes. God knows that they had enough loot from the shades to set up a hundred young men.

"Where did he say he had found it?" said one woman.

"Where," said a young knight, "was it before it was his?"

"He talked to the king—but the king did not *prattle* of such matters." Faces twitched as they realized that Marcus would not tell them. Some looked stunned, as if realizing he perhaps did not know. Cheerfully, he talked about the slaughter of the shades on its edge.

Sanchia walked on. For centuries, every second or third generation, the king had had to lead his men against the shades— and the creatures were of shadow. Even here, she had heard tales of their abilities to hide and ambush. No one could be sure of slaughtering them all.

Shouts sounded in the courtyard: Lord Alessandro returned. She took her place to receive him.

The company was vibrant with banners and tabards, in green and gold, scarlet and blue. Sanchia wondered if they had stopped, half a mile out, to make this brave show. She searched the crowd and hoped that five years could not have changed

Alessandro past recognition. And then, among the last men, he rode into the courtyard. He bore rather more travel-dust than any of his companions, and wore his coat of arms on his tabard: a golden dragon on a black background. He looked as somber among the men as she did among the women.

Well, thought Sanchia as he handed over his horse to the grooms, Alessandro also needed to make his authority clear. Her hands tightened on her skirt. He looked tired, but then, he had traveled far, to arrive on the day that he had promised.

He climbed the stairs into the great hall. Closer to him, Sanchia noted the lines on his face. His weariness was not all travel. She curtseyed. Alessandro bowed to kiss her hand, like the young knight she had wed, but this close, she could see a scar across his jaw, and the lines graven in his face.

"Welcome back, my lord. In view of your journey, I deferred the feast until dinner tomorrow—the supper is ready, but no great festivities until you and your men have rested."

Alessandro nodded, and seemed about to speak, but a whisper came from behind her: "What are you waiting for, children? Go greet your lord father."

The nurse put her hands on her charges' shoulders. Beatrice managed a curtsey before she bolted to hide her face in her mother's skirts. Rosa tilted her head to one side as she inspected Alessandro. She darted forward to touch his sleeve, as if to verify that he was there. Alessandro looked gravely at her, and Rosa pulled back to join her sister. Sanchia felt her daughters' grip on the clothing, and her tongue knotted.

Alessandro sighed, but so faintly that Sanchia was certain that only she heard it. He dropped to one knee. Sanchia thought of urging the girls forward, but they were frightened enough, even her bold little Rosa.

Alessandro merely spoke, telling them how pretty they were, and how glad he was to see them.

Beatrice looked up, her fingers tightening on Sanchia's skirt. "Is that the magic sword that Sir Marcus said you had?"

Alessandro smiled. It lit up his face, and Beatrice even loosened her grip.

"Would you like to see it, my Lady Beatrice?"

She considered a moment and let go, to step toward her father. Alessandro put his hands to her waist. "In your mother's solar, I may show you the sword in peace."

Beatrice did not protest as Alessandro picked her up and rose. He glanced at Rosa, and Sanchia picked her up to join him in the withdrawal. The great hall broke into babble behind them, as the curious engulfed the newcomers.

"All the new knights are eager to speak with the maidens," said Alessandro, and Sanchia remembered how few of the knights had been wed before they left.

The stair to the solar appeared ahead of them. Alessandro slowed. Sanchia looked at him, puzzled. He kept his new pace steadily, but shifted Beatrice to his left arm. Beatrice threw her arms about her father's neck as if nothing were wrong.

Perhaps nothing is, thought Sanchia. After five years, you can not expect to fathom all his thoughts.

The solar's three windows were enough light at the moment, but Sanchia reminded herself to have the candles lit as she let down Rosa.

Alessandro sat Beatrice on a chest, undid his sword belt, and sat. Rosa scurried over to stare at the scabbard. Sanchia sat, taking up her embroidery, as demurely as in the days when, their parents having agreed the match would be good, Alessandro had wooed her.

Alessandro said, "This is the enchanted sword I found in the mountains. It is a marvel. It slays shadows when no other blade can harm them." He told them of battles he had fought with it.

Rosa's finger traced the scabbard, and after a minute, Beatrice was bold enough to lay her hand on the hilt.

"Sir Marcus said that only you could draw it," said Rosa.

"Only I can," said Alessandro. "And I could not have, when I first left."

Sanchia blinked at that. The stories—some of them—said that only Alessandro could draw it, but not one said that he ever could not. She stitched, slowly. Then, he had not gained the sword at once.

"Now," said Rosa with glee, "you are a hero, and they make songs about you."

Alessandro nodded. Sanchia noted that he had not told them where it had come from, and who had had it before him.

His gaze went across the room. "But things have changed here as well. You wear not the bright colors that you used to, my lady."

"My lord, I dress like a sober and respectable matron," Sanchia said. "What else can a woman do, if she wishes for the respect of her lord's tenants?"

Rosa wriggled. "Father Gabriel said she should, 'cause she had no. . . cause to attract men, when you weren't here."

Sanchia felt herself coloring and could not meet her husband's gaze. No, she had not dressed to attract in his absence. The last thing she had wanted was young fools among her vassals and knights, but he had returned, and it was her duty to attract him.

"Then," she said decorously, "I received news of your arrival, which would not tarry for a new wardrobe."

Alessandro chuckled. "Indeed, it would not." He laid his sword aside and kissed his daughters on the forehead. "Go with your mother, my dears. I should bathe before supper."

Sanchia rose. "Ines will take charge of them. I will attend your bath."

Alessandro nodded and ran a hand through his hair. "Send up my squire while you are getting the bath, and I will disarm." He glanced sideways at her.

Sanchia directed the maids with the bathwater, and lit the candles about the room with the taper she had brought with her. The disarmed Alessandro sat on the chest.

She lit the last candle. "Beatrice and Rosa are regaling anyone who will listen with the tales of your sword."

"They are lovely children. You should be proud of them." Alessandro rose to his feet, and she came over to help him disrobe. "After Beatrice's birth, Flor said that a first birth was the hardest, that the next would be easier."

Sanchia's hands hesitated on his belt. How long it had been. His breath touched her cheek.

"Was Rosa's birth easier?"

Sanchia swallowed. "Not easy, perhaps, but easier." She undid his belt, and her hands remembered disrobing him. He smelled of the dusty road, and of horse—and of himself, which the years had not made less familiar.

She shook out his tunic. The candle flames swirled, and the shadows danced crazily. Alessandro stiffened. His hands shifted as if to reach for the sword. Slowly, she folded the tunic, eying him, and the shadows. Only when the movement had died down did he ease again.

Sanchia let out a long breath. "Did the shades strike as they pleased, my lord?" she said, tugging off his shirt.

"They would not have struck here—too much light." He shook his head. "To survive in light, they had to take form, and anyone could strike them down. They preferred shadowed rooms, where they could dissolve to nothingness before a blow."

Sanchia's eyelashes came down, hiding Alessandro's face from her. She remembered the stairway. He had slowed when they were about to walk into shadow.

"But," said Alessandro, with a briskness that seemed forced, "then I found the sword. That can strike a shade down wherever it appears. They can not vanish before it."

She wondered whether to ask how he had found it, but he bent his attention to his remaining clothing, as if to dismiss the matter. Five years, Sanchia thought, and swallowed.

The cloudy day shadowed the great hall, and she had sent for torches, but she could see clearly enough for now.

"Indeed, my lady," said Marcus glibly, "in the mountains we feared every shadow as an ambush, but the shades never came this far even at their worst." He beamed. "With your lord leading us, we ended them all, anyway."

Behind him, torches arrived, sending orange light to flood the room. She nodded dismissal, and Marcus bowed and headed across the room. A torch loomed behind him, and he jumped back from the shadow. She shook her head and walked across the floor, considering the kitchens.

Out of the corner of her eye, she saw a shadow lurch. She glanced about, and saw nothing that could have made it move like that—and no more untoward movements of shadows. Her breath came low and shallow.

Alessandro and the knights affected me, Sanchia thought. As soon as she finished with the kitchens, she would head for the solar, hoping some needlework would calm her.

Embroidery did not help. The castle folk seemed to notice no flaws in the lady of the manor, but every shadow drew her eye now. Even Alessandro did not seem as jumpy to her, when she descended to the great hall, still torch-lit, for dinner and the little masque after.

She lifted a wine cup and drank, trying to keep her gaze on the actors. Her maidens had made the costumes for the masque themselves, with remarkable speed, when the news first arrived, and now watched, bright-eyed with excitement.

Sanchia lowered her cup as a lion threatened to savage a princess. At first, she had wondered why the masque did not depicted the war just over, but now she was glad. She did not think she could have stood it.

Beatrice and Rosa bounced in excitement. Alessandro smiled at the masque. Then something loomed behind him. Her tongue froze in her mouth. I am imagining it, I am imagining it, it is like the shadow I dreamed I saw in the hall. . . .

The shadow leapt down and flooded over Alessandro. He barely had time to reach for his sword, and none to draw it, before it struck him down, and he collapsed against the chair. Screams pealed from her mouth. She barely heard them, her attention bent on the man before her. All about the hall, benches scrapped the floor as men leapt to their feet. The shadow flowed away, and Sanchia bent over Alessandro. His skin was clammy, but he still breathed.

Still breathed. She could not have told whether her heart hammered from panic or delight. Rosa screamed, and Beatrice, her face white, pushed by her to reach for her father.

Sanchia drew a deep breath. "Marcus, Honesto, Gregory! Bring your master to the great chamber." She looked for her maids. "Flor, bring candles." Many candles, she thought. Enough to keep the shadows slayable. She looked at the sword that her husband carried, and could draw. Unlike the rest of his men, who could only slay the shades in plentiful light. She swallowed. Many, many, many candles.

"It must have arrived last night," said Marcus, dully. "They travel by night. . . ."

Sanchia tugged on the bed's hangings, drawing them closer to the posts. She ought to have them taken down; they cast shadows in the candlelight. Alessandro, pale as bone, had not worsened, but he had not regained consciousness either. She forced her voice to keep steady. "Do the injured often die?"

Marcus shook his head. "Not those not killed at once—but it can take a long time to recover—"

"That is not so important," Sanchia said. She looked at Alessandro's sword. "He said that none of you could draw it, only him." Marcus nodded. "Show me."

Marcus gave her a strange look, and walked over to pull on the hilt. The blade did not move in its scabbard. "It had some strange name, about why not. . . I don't remember." He shook his head and laid down the sword. "You could not get the tale out of him though you plied him all night with wine."

Sanchia sighed. No matter the tale—she cared for the tale unfolding before her. "Send me Flor, and see about that message to the king." Marcus bowed. Sanchia watched him go, thinking bitterly that the king would do her or Alessandro no good, but would rage if he did not hear.

Then, she would not do Alessandro any good, though she lingered over him. Enough candles would keep the shade back, guards stood in the antechamber, and his lands had duties, even as they had when he fought in the mountains. Her fingers closed on a comb, on the table. She ought to have Flor prepare her a chamber. It would be folly to sleep here. She would only be in the way when his men fought the shade.

"I knew it," grumbled Flor in the hallway, her voice echoing strangely. "I knew they would bring trouble with them."

The comb hurtled through the air and smashed against the wall, inches from Flor's face. Her eyes bulged, and then she looked at Sanchia and cringed. Sanchia gave crisp orders to have a bed set up in the antechamber—and to clean up the pieces of the comb. Flor curtseyed and hurried off, and Sanchia forced herself to let out a long breath. However pettily Flor acted, that deed was unworthy of a lady. She walked over to the bed and looked down at Alessandro, still unmoving. At least I missed, she tried to console herself, and many a highborn lady would not have.

Beatrice and Rosa wanly pretended to play with their dolls in the corner of the great hall. Sanchia kissed their foreheads and told them it was bedtime.

"Will Father be all right?" Beatrice's fingers clenched the doll until she had nearly squeezed it in half.

"No worse," said Sanchia gravely. "Remember him in your prayers tonight."

Both girls' heads bobbed, their little faces solemn. Sanchia bit her lip. They had prayed for Alessandro's safety for so long, when he was at war. . . . She kissed them again and did not stop to watch them off. They should not have to be such good girls, she thought as she hurried up the stairs. She had hoped, with Alessandro home, that she would not have to leave them so much in the servants' hands.

Six men, all knights who had fought the shadows in the mountains, stood marshaled about the bed. The sky outside the window still showed scarlet and orange, and everything was ready for the night. She checked the supplies of candles and gave the men good night before retreating the antechamber, where the waiting bed only repelled her. She went to the window. A cool breeze came in, and the sound of the Angelus bell ringing. She said her prayers and listened as the last people settled in for the night. The sunset faded away, the moon had not risen, and she sat in the light of a single candle.

She wished she could stay in the great chamber, where the candlelight would let her do the finest embroidery, but the guards needed to have no fear of striking her. The breeze rose toward a wind. Sanchia shivered and rose to her feet. If she watched from the door, she could not get in the way. Picking up the candle, she rose to her feet. No sounds came from within the bedchamber. She walked over, sheltering her candle's flame with her hand.

Alessandro lay, unmoving, on the bed. The guards about him seemed almost as motionless. Sanchia wondered how long this could go on. The shade had struck down the great hero and might have retreated, satisfied, but she could not know that.

She studied his face, gilded by the candlelight. We can not live like this forever, Sanchia thought. Waiting for another strike. Setting men forever to guard his sleep. . . .

Why not? said a cold thought. She had waited for years for Alessandro's return. And she thought she could declare this wait too long when it had not lasted a day? She shivered.

The wind gusted. Sanchia, startled, moved her hand closer to the flame to shield it, and nearly burned herself. She had only a glimpse of the bed hangings swirling and the candle flames bending doubled and going out. The wind fell, and Sanchia, terrified, pulled back her hand from her candle. Shadow loomed over Alessandro.

"The shade!" bellowed a knight, and the swords leapt out. The shade unbent, as if looking at them. Sanchia slid behind the knights, relighting the candles, and when the lights flared up, the shade vanished. She did not pause, but went on to the next candle, and the next. When a knight looked to take the candle from her, she shook her head.

"Keep guard," she said.

Sanchia sat by the bed, clasping her husband's cold hand. The candles were all relit. The smell of burning beeswax was slowly replacing the damp night air. The bed hangings, off the bed, hung over the windows, against the wind. Her grip tightened. Alessandro still breathed, she tried to console herself. A sideways glance showed her his gray face. His breath was lighter than it had been, and his heart beat less strongly. The shade could only come a few more times, and the hero would die.

I ought to sleep, Sanchia thought. I will need to think in the morning. The lands will not come to a halt because their lord was dying, any more than when he was absent. And I have to devise some way to keep the shade *out*.

She started to lay down Alessandro's hand, and could not. With a sigh, she leaned against the bed.

"I will praise you, Lord." The altar boy's voice rang sweetly in the psalm. "You have rescued me, and have not let my enemies rejoice over me."

Sanchia knelt in the chapel. Beatrice and Rosa pressed close to either side of her, and she could not attend to the service. Her thoughts flew away in unformed guesses about what could be done—though Marcus, Honesto, and all the others who had fought the shades were as baffled as she was.

The altar boy sang on. "Lord, you brought me up from the grave; you kept me from those going down into the pit."

Sanchia swallowed and tried to attend. A long time later, the service finished, and she joined the people filing out of it. She garnered more glances. One peasant muttered, about a babe, and her mouth tightened. She might be with child now, and it was too soon to abandon hope of her conceiving. Alessandro was not dead. She felt a strange twist to her stomach. If he did die, an infant heir would be little better than two girl orphans and a widow: all would fall under the king's wardship.

The king, thought Sanchia, will not allow his hero's widow and children to suffer. Beatrice pulled closer to her, and Sanchia put her arm about her. Dear God, let the king be generous with his hero's widow and children.

Rosa tugged on her sleeve. "Why couldn't Father's sword kill the shade?"

"Only Father. . . ." Sanchia stopped. Alessandro had told the girls that once, he could not draw the sword. If all the knights *had been* unable to draw it—perhaps they could now.

"Are you certain of this, my lady?" said Marcus.

Sanchia looked at the knights gathering in the courtyard. No, they were not all knights; many were men-at-arms, and they included those who had remained behind, during the war. "I myself heard my lord husband tell my daughters that he could not always draw the sword. That no one else could before does not mean that no one else can, now."

The knights jostled the men-at-arms to the end of the line, and among themselves for places. Sanchia's smile faded—but let one of them draw the sword and kill the shade, and she would forgive him everything.

The men-at-arms were not leaving, she noted.

"The glory of slaying the last shade would draw them," Marcus said. "King Gaspar will be pleased—if a little embarrassed that he declared them annihilated before."

Sanchia snorted. "He should have learned circumspection as his grandfather had." Marcus blinked. "King Mergildo had declared the shades driven back. He had learned that kings before him had declared the shades gone, and they had always returned to haunt the land."

She walked across the courtyard, with the sword. The first knight tried to draw it. When it did not slide out, he wrapped one hand about the scabbard, the other about the hilt and yanked. It did not move.

Sanchia retreated to the great hall, to stand in the shadow of its arched doorway, half-hidden as she watched. She did not think she could watch before them all.

"He told us, too, that he could not always draw it," said Honesto, his lined face looking more wearied than ever. He watched the men-at-arms trying to draw the sword.

Sanchia nodded. The knights had all tried, and most of the men-at-arms, and she was losing hope. She glanced at Honesto again. He looked deeply grieved. She had not remembered for years, that Honesto had trained Alessandro in swordplay.

"He had some story about it—none of us paid much heed—he staggered back with that sword, he had not slept in two days it seemed—he babbled, and we thought he was off his head—but after he slept, he no longer wanted to talk." Honesto hesitated. "Once he used it in battle, we cared."

The last man tried to draw the sword. The extent to which her heart sank startled Sanchia.

The sun set in fiery pinks and yellows. In the courtyard, the knights prepared themselves for their watch. Sanchia watched them longer than she should have but finally tore herself away to give orders to the maids about the candles and the bed hangings—taken down to admit the sunlight, but now needed against night winds. The maids scurried off to prepare.

Alessandro muttered. Sanchia stood in the doorway, telling herself that she hoped too much, he could not have recovered after two attacks. Then his head rolled to one side. She bolted to the bed. "Shush, my darling, my darling." His hand reached toward her, and she snatched it up. It felt only a little warmer than before, but her heart hammered. "You are too ill, you must rest, do not. . . ."

"Sanchia. . . sword. . . ." His eyes shifted as he tried to search the room.

"It's here, my lord," she said, wondering what he was about. He could not think that he could fight. She tried to pull her hand free, to show him it. Alessandro's hand tightened on hers with startling strength. "*Sword.*"

His expression was fierce—he knew something important— but she could not read it. "I tried the other knights. . . ."

"No." Alessandro shook his head. "Not what I. . . ." And then he fell back on his pillow.

Sanchia watched him a long time. His fingers lay limp in hers again, and she laid his hand down without rousing him. The sword was. . . she looked about the room and walked over to retrieve the sword from the chest. She could show him, if he recovered again, even if it would do no good against the shade. She picked the blade up. The hilt and scabbard alike were plain, the pommel metal rather than the gemstones that even poor lords affected.

Who needs a gemstone when all the land knows the sword is magic? thought Sanchia. When it can not be drawn, even to save its master's life? The sunset let less light into the room than she had realized. Scowling, she brought the blade under the candles to inspect it. A sword that no one could draw—she put her hand to the hilt, and tugged at it.

It moved.

Sanchia stared at it. Candlelight glinted from the exposed metal, little though it was. She had drawn it, not just fancied she had in her desperation. Her heart pounding, she shoved it back it in, and her fingers clenched the sword. Why her? Why her? She could not fight with it—and she did not doubt that disaster would ensue if she drew the sword and gave another knight it.

The candles slowly burned. How difficult could it be? she thought. The shade did not have a sword of its own. She looked at the bed and walked over. The shade could not expect her to draw the sword. She would have a moment, though only a moment, when she could strike without fear.

She let out a long breath. The maids would be here any moment, with the candles, and to cover the windows. She had to decide now. She turned toward the door, and saw a shadow move.

Night has not fallen, she thought.

The shade loomed up on the wall, vivid in the scarlet light, and swooped through the candlelight, past her, toward Alessandro—as if it had learned the knights would guard Alessandro after dark, and come early to avoid them.

Alessandro groaned. Sanchia leapt for the sword. Her hands fumbled with it as if they had forgotten to hold things, and it slid to the floor. Sanchia dropped to her knees, put one hand on the scabbard, and drew the sword with the other. It glittered in the candlelight, and Sanchia rose, watching the shade as it loomed over Alessandro. No face, no eyes marked that form, but it seemed utterly intent on him. Her mouth set. She lifted the sword and struck out, directly through the shade.

It screamed—a high-pitched, strange sound. Shouts came from below and, moments later, the hammer of footsteps on the stairs. The shade writhed on the sword. The door was thrown open to bang on the wall opposite, and the wind sent all the candle flames dancing and blew the shade away to nothingness.

"My lady!" Marcus gawked.

Sanchia lowered the sword. There was writing on the blade, and she lifted it to read: *Nolo esse heros.* She looked at her husband again, where he lay as still as before, and whispered, "I do not want to be a hero?"

Alessandro did not even suggest that he might rise in the morning, but the chill had gone from his body, his face had regained its color, and when Beatrice and Rosa intruded with their dolls, Alessandro laughed and admired the dolls until Sanchia ushered the girls off, to play in the corner.

Alessandro looked at her. "Are all the petitioners gathering for the manor court?"

Sanchia picked up her embroidery and did not look up from it. "Yes. And they are plentiful. Many of them I have seen before, over these years."

Alessandro laughed, deep in his throat. "They think I will overrule your decisions—they will be shocked when you must hold it still, this time."

In the silence after, Sanchia looked at her stitches. It felt like many a morning had, before he had left, but it was not same. "On the sword—does the inscription mean I do not want to be a hero?"

"Even so," said Alessandro. "Not all the years of hunting down shades in the mountains could dissuade the young knights from wishing to be a hero. But I. . . ." He laughed, shortly. "Not at first. I was willing to be a hero then, and that was why I could not have drawn the sword."

Her heart beat faster. She had reminded herself, often, that the king had summoned Alessandro. She glanced at him. She had not, she supposed, really believed it.

"But after two years—I had a wife, I had two daughters, one of whom I had never seen." He shook his head.

Sanchia smiled. "How did you find it?" she said.

"On a grave." He glanced at her. "I had never heard of the man buried there."

"He must have been a wise man," said Sanchia. "He did not want to be a hero."

Eyes of the Sorceress

Sounds filtered in from the army's camp, but Apollonia studied the table instead of the tent's entrance. She did not want to look a nervous fool in Captain Florian's eyes. Ever. But especially not when she cast a spell on him.

The vast tent held only her and the table; the table held a bronze neckring with two opaque blue stones, and a pale blue crystal like a platter. In the light seeping through the canvas, they gleamed. Apollonia pressed her hands to her sides, to keep from shifting the stones. Again.

"In here," said Bianca, the Royal Mistress of Sorceresses, her voice low and demure.

A man entered. He wore the green of the royal army, but also royal violet, and Apollonia felt blood leaching from her face. Built like a bull, his face set in harsh lines, a man reuniting a kingdom torn by sorcery and swords for a century. On a crucial campaign—and her spell would help—she hoped.

Her hands feeling like wood, Apollonia made her curtsey.

"Which one is this?" said King Magnus.

"Apollonia," said Bianca, as if it was of no importance.

Given the way King Magnus looked past her, Apollonia suspected the king would not remember her the thousandth time he saw her, though Bianca presented her every time.

Apollonia let her breath out. He would not see her a thousand times. Her spellcraft was useful too seldom. So it befitted her to cast it well, those rare times. She truly did not want to look like a fool before the king.

Captain Florian had come in while her wits had wandered—and guards and attendants enough to fill up the tent that had

seemed so large. Apollonia looked at the table to keep from
gawking. She had no wish to appear thoughtless, unable to cast a
vital spell. Though—she straightened—for this spell, the king
had no choice. Dozens of sorceresses traveled with the army, but
not one other who could cast this.

Captain Florian nodded to her, as courteously as to a great
noblewoman. Then, King Magnus had chosen the fair-spoken
Captain Florian as his emissary for good reason.

Apollonia took up the bronze neckring. Captain Florian bent
his head and let her put it on him.

"Close your eyes," she said. "And keep them closed."

He eyed her as if he had not really noticed her before, but
obeyed. Apollonia touched his eyelids and was glad that she had
mastered the spell; it slid from her mouth without any trace of
her nerves.

For a moment after, she stood still. This aspect of the spell
she always disliked: the slippery sensations that the eyestones
lent her, down to feeling her own fingers as if they touched her
own eyelids. She forced back the distraction and lowered her
hand. Her own eyelids felt the fingers leave.

She returned to the table, to cast the second spell on the stone
there. That one was short, and in moments, the crystal went
dark.

"Open your eyes, Captain," she said.

The crystal flooded with light, and in tiny form, it showed the
tent, the king and his attendants, Bianca in her gray robe, and a
colorless sorceress in a gray robe, her drab blond hair floating
free—and no wonder no one heeded a mouse like her.

Apollonia crept to the corner as they talked. Being a mouse in
the encampment was no bad thing.

King Magnus laughed with Captain Florian. His honor
guard, with the flag of parley, stood arrayed outside, ready to
bring him to the castle. King Magnus touched Captain Florian's
shoulder and told him to win the battle without a blow.

Captain Florian laughed. "That will be the day. But, Your Majesty, he will have his chance."

Apollonia let her breath out. They would not need her until they wanted the spell broken, but to leave for the sorceresses' tent would attract attention. And she had entered the king's service to help reunite the kingdom, not to listen to Emma's jibes about how she wasn't needed for long.

She did not watch the crystal as Captain Florian left the tent and mounted; that always made her seasick, watching, but then the horses rode off. The crystal showed grass and the duke's keep, the dark stone still small with distance, sitting where it guarded the only pass through the mountains about them. Which made it so vital to the king.

Captain Florian's horse was restive. Apollonia felt it shifting through the spell and swallowed. Queasiness would only make her task more difficult, but she could endure it. Up the slope— up and up, with white and violet flowers growing low on the ground to either side. No trees grew, this high in the mountains, where the winds blew so sharply.

She heard the voices as they arrived at the castle, and the guards received them with outward courtesy: Captain Florian's as if she herself spoke; the duke's rumble and the voices of his men; and all the voices, redoubled by the crystal as King Magnus watched. The duke's castle was dark, the tapestries hung on the wall were old, but his men wore fine armor, standing to either side of the white bearded duke, slumped and scowling in his ornate carved chair of dark wood.

Gravely, Captain Florian spoke of how, despite the chaos, the duchy still formed part of the kingdom.

"With a king who practices sorcery," said the duke. "Sorcery that tore the kingdom apart."

"Swords did much as sorcery to tear the kingdom apart, Your Grace. Yet you do not disarm your men."

"When you bring battle to me? What profit would it bring me to disarm them?"

"To welcome the king? The land prospers under his reign. Bandits have been suppressed—"

"And tax collectors flourish."

Apollonia's hands jerked at the sneer in his voice. Did he not even *care* about bandits? She forced her breath in and out.

"Do you think I have not heard of your king's army? Not nobles, not even knights. Mercenaries. Paid in *land*."

"King Magnus brought peace to the land, suppressed bandits, and made wilds safe. Few veterans are with the army, but fewer still hold lands that other men held, and only when they forced the king to force them from their lands. Most soldiers hold where rack and ruin had driven all peaceable men from holdings."

"Baseborn peasants, holding lands like the gently born." The duke eyed him. "Sending one like *you* to parley with me."

"I am the son of a duke, and the brother of a duke," said Florian, his voice measured, but Apollonia felt the tension in his body. She glanced at King Magnus; he seemed to have seen nothing. Perhaps she imagined it.

"My brother has no complaint of how the king treated him. Throughout the realm, the king confirmed in their places—and rewarded!—those who kept peace and administered justice. There is no need for war, when there can be peace and honor."

"When your *king* offers me a place as his lackey? Like some fat merchant—your *king* will regard me and any whining merchant as alike, beneath him."

Captain Florian shifted his weight. King Magnus's eyes narrowed.

"Guards!" shouted the duke. "Show them the difference between my men and merchants who complain of the toll!"

Apollonia saw steel glint, and men fall; she smelled blood. Hands grabbed arms—as if her arms, as if to hold her. She felt as if a sword fell from her hand, and realized she had felt the hilt in

Captain Florian's. Too quick to be clearly seen, something came toward the face—

All went black in bitter pain.

Apollonia shook her head. Her eyes had squeezed shut without her even noticing the motion, and her stomach roiled. Shouts sounded about her. Not the duke's, she knew, not the duke's men—a minute later, feeling as if she had aged where she stood, she forced her eyes open.

The crystal had turned black. Dependent on *his* eyes, thought Apollonia, dully. King Magnus, on his feet, shouted orders loud enough to half-deafen them, and his men ran about him. Bianca, like a maidservant, grabbed the crystal and scurried aside.

Apollonia shook her head again and regretted it as her stomach heaved. She had to get out of the way; they had less interest in her than in Bianca. She had to leave, even if she crawled under the canvas—but her eyes hurt, and if she moved foolishly, her stomach would revolt.

She stood, shivering. She could imagine the duke saying filthy sorcery. . . .

"What are you doing here?" A lieutenant roared over her. "With battles to be fought and deaths to be avenged, how dare you clutter up the tent?"

His hand came down on her shoulder, shoving her.

At the motion, her stomach heaved again. Apollonia retched until her stomach was empty—and, futilely, painfully, retched on after.

People in the tent stared. Bianca looked torn between fury and cowering. King Magnus looked as furious as he had since Captain Florian fell—but his gaze was on the lieutenant.

"Have you nothing to do, lieutenant? When your superior was treacherously murdered before your very eyes? You have nothing to do but attack a woman who did you no harm?"

The sorceresses' tent was dim. By the entrance, where the daylight fell, the others gossiped as they sewed, but it was still quieter than the king's command tent.

"I heard," said Emma, "that the king was not pleased with Lieutenant Simon."

The squeals were louder. "I can't—with the *lieutenant*? —just a sorceress like us—"

Apollonia, cold and shivery, pulled the pillow over her head. Her eyes ached, and weak tears trickled down her face. She wished the king would be not pleased with *them*.

The sorceresses chattered on about Lieutenant Simon. What idiots, thought Apollonia. The king only shouted at him because he was there, and the king was angry.

About the tent, the army bustled.

Apollonia closed her eyes. They might need her sorcery in the attack. It would be the first time, but they might. She should rest and recover for that. At least, she should try—

"Emma," said Bianca, harshly. "All of you. *Mending* when there's a siege?"

Among the rustles as they rose, one said, "Apollonia?"

"We don't need her."

Apollonia's mouth twitched, but she could not complain. With the chatter gone, she closed her eyes and tried to sleep.

Apollonia woke abruptly in gloom, her thoughts murky with ghastly dream remnants. She shook her head and sat up but could not shake out the rest. A vile dream, to stick so long even as she woke, though nothing more than fragments of taunts. Undermining, oil, siege weapons—all things she had heard of, traveling with the army, but none that made sense.

She dragged in a deep breath. At least she had slept. For hours—outside, fires blazed, and cold air flooded the tent.

She crept from her cot, straightened her clothes, and passed a comb through her hair. Outside, the full moon had risen almost to zenith, but the other sorceresses had not returned. They must have proven useful.

She took up her mantle and eased among the tents. She had missed dinner; she wondered how many, soldier or sorceress, had. The soldiers had loved Captain Florian, and the king had cherished him like a son.

At the cooking tents, she scrounged bread and cheese—and even soup, when one cook said that the king had been angry with Lieutenant Simon over her.

"Said that he should be angry with the duke and not the lassie," grumbled the other cook, "nothing more," but Apollonia got her soup. She ate, wondering whether she would be known throughout the camp for that.

Even a full stomach did not shake the dream from memory. Through the cool air, she slid through the camp, evading the paths of soldiers as they prepared for the attack. She had never seen such grim faces, even after a battle. Then, while battles killed more men, they did not die by such treachery.

She wandered past the last tents. She could stay out from underfoot out in the fields as well as in the camp. For a moment, she remembered Captain Florian's path, over this same grass, before it was wet with dew. She swallowed. Even in the gloom, the ducal keep seemed to loom overhead.

The sound of digging drew her attention from the keep, and she scowled. It felt odd to her, though she could not put her finger on why. Not even when she saw low lanterns, and men digging toward a tower, with two sorceresses standing over them. Bertha and Claudette—sorceresses of earth—she wondered whether the tunnel had gotten farther than it looked, if they had used sorcery on it.

Serious men watched the digging; one was King Magnus, who spoke in a low voice with the others, about the tower. Frowning, Apollonia listened, until she was certain.

"You are going to undermine the south tower," she said—louder than she intended. Baleful glances came from all about. King Magnus's eyes narrowed as he glared at the impudent little mouse who interrupted him. She cringed; a minute of that gaze would sap her will.

So she had to act before that minute.

"Then, Your Majesty, I know two things for your ear alone."

Before guards could move, she crossed the earth, heedless of the uneven footing. She was here to serve him, not to avoid attention, she reminded herself. She fought down the impulse to bite her lip and came close enough to whisper.

"Your Majesty, the duke knows of what you are doing, and is readying ensorcelled oil to welcome you, and—" She lowered her voice further. "Captain Florian is alive."

Even with the torchlight coloring his face with orange and gold, she could see how he paled.

Two soldiers carried the torches to either side, sending shadows dancing whenever soldiers or sorceresses hurried from their way. Bianca hurried and muttered under her breath—inaudibly since she had told Apollonia to keep up. Apollonia scurried along, her skirts gathered in her hands to keep from tripping, not daring to walk too far behind the king for fear of being caught by the crowd—and the king moved at a fearful pace.

She had time to see the glances she garnered.

The royal tent stood strides from any other, despite the silencing sorcery on the cloth. King Magnus ordered guards to allow no one close. They nodded in obedient silence but glanced at her as she passed within. The torchmen stayed outside.

Inside, three candles sat on a small table, burning swan-white flames that cast almost as much shadow as light. The king dropped into the chair and turned to her.

"Tell me."

Bianca, by the entrance, had come no farther and looked disapproving. Her face was so severe it was hard to remember that she was only a decade or two older than her charges.

Apollonia reminded herself that it did not matter what Bianca thought. She had followed the king in on his orders.

"I had thought that I suffered because the spell broke, and because of the captain's death,"—the king's mouth twisted—"but I dreamed of taunts. Saying the army dug under the south tower, and he had oil to greet them."

"You troubled the king for nothing," said Bianca, folding her arms. "We all saw the crystal go black."

The king's eyebrows went up, and he sat back, as if waiting. He had not even glanced at Bianca.

And Apollonia had to concede, it was a good question.

"You saw it go black before. When I first cast the spell."

Bianca's lip curled. "Do you think Captain Florian closed his eyes in the middle of a fight?"

"I think he was blinded in the middle of a fight. My eyes hurt." Her hand twitched. "They still do."

King Magnus's eyes narrowed.

"We all *heard* it," said Bianca. "The eye was only part of it. We heard the parley."

"The eye was primary, for *that one*," said Apollonia. "The other spell—I must make myself a conduit for the crystal. That spell had rather less need for the eye."

Bianca snorted. "But it did need that neckring. The duke left it on him?"

"He would have, if he thought it—" She pronounced the words carefully. "—'Filthy sorcery.'" She glanced at King Magnus. He glanced between them. "I did not realize it as the time, I was too shaken, but I heard the duke say that after—the crystal went dark. He would not want his men tainted by its touch." She drew a deep breath. "I heard the rest more clearly: the oil and all."

Bianca drew herself up to her full height. "You talk nonsense. *Oil*? For the tunnel? Will they pour it on the soldiers' heads?"

"It can be used," said King Magnus, his voice measured, his attention on Bianca. "If ensorcelled properly. They did at Graystead."

For all the duke's contempt for sorcery. Apollonia's mouth twitched.

"So Mistress—" He glanced at her.

"Apollonia," she said, meekly. Mistress? One of the common sorceresses?

Bianca's face set, as if she were marshaling words.

"How did I know that the tower was being undermined?" said Apollonia, with more contempt than she had known she could muster. "Am I a mistress of siege works? I do not even know any spells that can be used to aid in them. How did I know that ensorcelled oil might be used against it? I wasn't at Graystead."

Bianca's mouth opened. Then it shut again. She looked haggard and years older than she had, moments before.

Apollonia faced the king. He studied Bianca again, but, from his face, he was realizing that Bianca believed her. That she spoke the truth.

King Magnus winced. His eyes shut. For a minute, he looked unable to speak. Then, heavily, he said, "This news must not escape. No one must know that Captain Florian is alive."

Apollonia wondered if the king would rather he had died than remained alive, beyond rescue, in agony. She felt her eyes hurt, and a thousand more pains. The spell did not even carry injuries well.

"Mistress Apollonia, bring news at once, if you dream again." King Magnus rose. "I will order that you be admitted."

Apollonia curtseyed. "But not to say what I came for until you order it? In case there are captains or servants about?"

"Even so—prudent child."

As the king went toward the door, she felt a cold weight in her stomach. She *had* spoken to the king before them all, with no leave—

"In the night? If I must rouse you? I woke less than an hour ago."

"Night or day. No more of my men must fall when I could prevent it."

She curtseyed again. When she straightened, the king still studied her.

"Did you come from the lands my father held?" he said.

"No, Your Majesty," said Apollonia. "From Greenleaf. A village near Kingsport. I was old enough to remember when Your Majesty took the lands."

King Magnus snorted. Apollonia looked at her hands.

"And your family was glad of that?"

"My grandmother was, Your Majesty. She raised me." Apollonia straightened. "Her husband, all her children, and all her other grandchildren, had died in a bandit attack."

King Magnus nodded. Apollonia curtseyed and left. Her hands formed fists. She had been old enough to remember the bandit attack, too. Whatever the duke said, bandits lurked about these mountains. *He* had not put them down.

In the morning, Apollonia drifted about the encampment. Now that she knew them, Captain Florian's injuries insisted on being felt, and beyond them, an anguish that sprung from no wound. Then, he must have known that his escort had died. She watched the preparations to avenge him, perhaps even to free him, and ached all the same.

With evening, she went back to her cot.

When she woke again, even before reaching for shoes or mantle, she pulled back the tent flap and looked at the moon: near zenith again. She dragged in a breath of the night air, but the chill did not shake the dream, or the anguish.

Other sorceresses stirred and grumbled. Apollonia donned her shoes, grabbed her mantle, and scurried off, over ground wet with dew. At the king's tent, the guards raised their spears. One declared that the king had retired.

"At any hour," said Apollonia.

"He ordered—" said one, hesitantly.

"*Her*?" Another guard ducked, as if trying to see her face.

"I can shout," said Apollonia, sweetly. "And rouse everyone nearby. That will wake him. The silence spell keeps sounds within; it does not mean they can not reach him from outside."

Moments later, she ducked inside. A single candle shed less light than the moon, and she doubted that the king could make out her face. She told him that the duke would send men out the north-east postern gate, to raid the army.

King Magnus looked to the guards. "Send for Lieutenant Sebastian. He will lead a party to gather wood there and notice the raid." He smiled, smugly. "The duke will never know what betrayed him."

Apollonia, yawning, staggered over to the cooking tent as the sky to the east glowed in delicate roses and yellows. The other sorceresses looked up, said nothing as she took her bowl of porridge, and turned back to grumbling about tasks that probably would not even help take the fortress.

Apollonia took a seat and put down her bowl. "Emma, I need a soporific."

Emma looked up from her porridge. "You haven't had trouble sleeping."

"I need a soporific," said Apollonia. "Not a heavy one. Enough to make me sleep at noon, but wake by sunset."

Emma scowled at her, but did not start her sneers about how some sorceresses had little to do. Then, since they had not attacked the keep, Emma had no wounded to tend.

And Emma had to know that Apollonia talked with the king, late at night.

"And the sooner I get it," Apollonia said, putting down her spoon, "the better."

"Such a *specific* potion," Emma muttered into her bowl.

Sunset blossomed hot pink and pale orange. Apollonia, sitting on a stool, thought that might have been too early. The last two nights, she had woken about midnight; now she had to wait out the hours from sunset till then.

Better too early than too late. And was waiting out the night worse than waiting out the day?

She rose and, despite her aches and pains seeming to have worsen while she slept, she circled the tent and tried not to think about what Captain Florian suffered. Sunset darkened to violet, and then to black. Sorceresses came to their cots, glancing at her, but when she merely looked back, went on to their rest. Stars came out; the moon rose, enormous and reddish bronze. Drunken soldiers ambled by, and Apollonia whispered a spell. When one claimed to have seen something, they jeered, and he admitted that he saw nothing, now.

"Some sorceresses," she whispered, "have mastered spells of eyes."

She walked about the tent again. The night was so dreary that even the chill could not easily keep her awake.

Nor aches in her arms and her eyes. Chains, she thought, chaffing her wrists, and wondered how, even with Emma's potion, she had managed to sleep. And the anguish. She wondered if night or the cold or moonlight had somehow strengthened the sorcery; it felt like a stab to the heart. And she wondered if Captain Florian had managed to sleep at all.

She had not told the king that the spell might break at any time. No spell lasted forever, and most broke within days. She had never even heard of this one's being used as she used it. And whether its breaking would be easy—she eyed the moon, barely over the horizon, large, looming, still bronze in shade, but shrinking and paling with time. She had never seen a spell this large, breaking. Even the most foolish of sorceresses would dissipate her spells before they came to that point.

If they were not quite so foolish as she was.

The moon inched upward, to form a small, pale pearl against the starry sky. Every time she circled the tent, the dew lay more thickly on the grass, until her walks left her shoes and hem soaked.

When the moon reached its height, she sat with her hands folded in her lap. She heard—and did not hear—a door opening. A heavy door. She closed her eyes to listen.

Words came, vaguely. Taunts about how many of King Magnus's men had died that day, assurances that sorties from the postern gate would catch the army off guard.

Perhaps Captain Florian had twitched then, realizing that the promised sortie had not brought the promised slaughter. The voice snarled, and Apollonia knew it for the duke's.

"What do you think happened to *your* men?"

The anguish stabbed again. Clearly and distinctly, so close to the way she had felt after the bandits' attack.

Minutes later, silence came. A door thudded shut, and silence reigned again. She wondered if Captain Florian wept.

She stood. The night breezes were cold despite her gown and mantle. Her tongue touched her lip. The king had ordered her to come if she dreamed, not if she learned anything useful.

"They—" King Magnus shook his head. "The duke would not have preserved them. Only Captain Florian would have value as a hostage in his eyes."

"They weren't fat merchants," whispered Apollonia. The guards eyed her. If King Magnus grew angry at this fruitless interruption, they would hustle her out.

"Do not rouse your hopes, Mistress Apollonia," said King Magnus.

Apollonia looked down. "I have thought. I heard the shovels before I saw them, two days ago." The king scowled, and she raised a hand. "Before I came into earshot—they were oddly familiar. And I heard other noises. Captain Florian is dungeoned in the south tower. Deep in it, but within."

King Magnus sighed. "Would that the knowledge could do me any good."

Apollonia twitched. "But—" She stopped and forced her voice down. "He could be found there."

King Magnus's face twisted as if she stabbed him. "Would that I could. I could not love Captain Florian more were he my son. And soon or late, he will die at the duke's hands. But I can not sacrifice so many men—so many father's sons—without bringing down the duke. Captain Florian has no—tactical importance."

"You know where the duke is, one hour a night," said Apollonia. "He is of tactical importance."

King Magnus's eyes narrowed.

"How close did the tunnel get to the tower?"

"They will see them coming," said King Magnus.

Apollonia raised a hand. "Look." She cast her spell again. When the king scowled, she broke it.

"So," King Magnus mused, "you cast this on soldiers—"

Apollonia shook her head. "I must go with them. Then, I can cast it on soldiers and myself, but I have to see. That is why I have not used it throughout this campaign."

King Magnus studied her.

"That is why Mistress Bianca did not have me spy on the castle with the crystal, because I could not see inside to cast the spell. Only when I cast it on Captain Florian, and he bore it inside—and this is worse. I have to go with them."

The king scowled. Her hands clasped, Apollonia waited. She had been a fool to study sorcery of the eye; she should have realized why it was so rare a study.

The king's voice was almost a growl in its discontent. "How close do you have to keep to them?"

They carried no lights; her spell could not hide that much, and so they crept by moonlight.

Lieutenant Sebastian said nothing to her. Apollonia was glad; whatever his questions, she doubted that she had answers. Sneaking into the tower unnerved her more than she dared show, but the soldiers knew she had proposed this venture. If she seemed nervous. . . .

The postern gate stood ahead. Apollonia laid her hand on Lieutenant Sebastian's wrist, staying him, and cast her spell. A guard turned. Lieutenant Sebastian leapt forward; Apollonia heard the footsteps and felt the air move. She looked away.

Even when a hand on her arm drew her forward, she tried not to look at the dead guards, or the dark blood spread about them. She told herself, carefully, that they might have cut down Captain Florian's men. She swallowed. Treacherously.

But she could not look.

Once within the tower, they descended, the air cooling as they went below the ground. On the bottom floor, with great stones of the foundation to either side, they reached a torch-lit corridor. There, a figure walked ahead of them, toward a cell. He held a key in hand.

Apollonia let her breath out. Wait, she thought. Let us check which cell holds the captain. Let him open the door so we can retrieve the captain—

But a soldier ran, and her spell could deceive only the eye. Footsteps hammered, and the duke, with a grunt, turned. Too much knowledge—the spell dissolved, and the duke looked at them all. Apollonia ducked against the wall. The other soldiers ran after, even Lieutenant Sebastian, and swords glinted by torchlight. The duke drew his own blade and fled down the corridor. Apollonia scurried after.

Lieutenant Sebastian struck, and the duke stopped to fight. Apollonia stood as far away as she could, until the key went flying. The duke lunged for it, but the soldiers barred his way. Apollonia drew a deep breath and cast the spell again, on herself alone. Ducking about the fight, she snatched up the key and ran. Her footsteps broke the spell again, but the duke had no chance to chase her.

The door opened under her hands, and behind it, the cell held a chained man. He raised his head—blood had dried on his cheeks—and turned away, as if remembering his blindness only after he had tried to look.

The duke shrieked in fury. He broke free, though he took a blow as he did, and ran toward her and the cell, dripping a brilliant red trail. The soldiers' pursuit, moments after, could not catch up.

Looking for a hostage, perhaps, or two. Or—Apollonia looked at his face—to ensure they did not rescue the captain.

Apollonia dropped to her knees, and her hand went to Captain Florian's throat, where the eyestones rested. Quickly as water spilling, Apollonia cast another spell, to reversing her first sorcery: not from him to her, from her to him.

Aches vanished as if washed away. Captain Florian sat, as if still assimilating that he could stare at the duke.

"Use the chains," whispered Apollonia. "They're heavy enough." Captain Florian surged to his feet as the duke reached him. He raised his left hand and tangled the duke's sword in its chain. The duke snarled and yanked at its hilt.

Captain Florian's right hand lashed out. Its chain connected with the duke's skull.

The blow was solid.

Apollonia, holding her breath, still waited until the body fell, armor striking against the stone, and sword clattering, and lay still, bleeding only a little blood, darker red than other blood she had seen, before she let drop the spell.

Captain Florian's hand went his head. She stepped forward with the key.

Night air buffeted them with chill as they crossed the grass. Captain Florian staggered along, his arm weighing like iron on her shoulders; another soldier held his other arm, but Lieutenant Sebastian had not wanted another soldier unready to fight, when the captain could walk well enough with that much aid.

Apollonia glanced back at the keep and let her spell drop, so they were seen.

A soldier shouted; she could not hear what. Then, the moonlight and firelight were enough to make them visible. To see soldiers appear before them, one lugging a corpse, and with a sorceress and a soldier supporting a bloodied man, would draw attention.

A crowd swarmed, gawking at the duke's corpse, and at Captain Florian, leaning harder on her and the soldier, his head hanging.

"Emma!" Apollonia shouted.

"Bring the body over here," shouted Lieutenant Sebastian. Soldiers lugged the corpse away, and some of the crowd followed. Emma pushed forward and stared at Captain Florian as she had not believed the stories.

"Do you want to tend him now?" said Apollonia. "Or can he safely be carried to a tent first?"

Emma eyed his wounds. "To the tent. They will not worsen for that." She shook her head. "Though nothing can be done for his eyes."

Apollonia's tongue touched her lips.

In the tent, with day illuminating it with ivory-colored light, Apollonia sat with her book in her lap and the eyestones lying before her. The siege went on, outside, but the noise was muffled and distant, and she was not needed for that. Here, though. . . . A convoluted spell, and one she had not cast before—she read it again.

But with the eyestones so close, they did not need true eyes. She forced her breath in and out. All she needed was a reversal. What had gone from the eyes to the stone could go the other way, and she did not even need to devise it herself.

"Mistress Apollonia?" Captain Florian's voice rose from the cot.

"Yes?" she said.

"I am not surprised that Mistress Emma hovers"—his voice was dry—"but I must confess that I do not know why you do."

"Readying a spell," said Apollonia. She wished she could test it, but the only way to see if it worked was to use it in truth. "I will cast it now."

She took up the bronze neckring and went to put it back about his neck.

He fingered it and grunted in surprise. "I saw this once."

"So you have," said Apollonia. Her tongue touched her lips. If she told him, the spell might not work and so dash his hopes—no, she would let him learn what it did after.

"And I wonder that you endured the spell, after I felt it in the dungeon." His face turned toward her.

"This is different."

After a moment, he lay back in silence.

Apollonia cast it. It only worked at such short range that she wondered that it had ever been devised. But since it worked the stones directly. . . .

Captain Florian studied her. A minute later, he said, "It's not your eyes, it can't be when I can see you. . . . "

Apollonia giggled, feeling light-headed with success. Deliberately posing before him, she closed her eyes and clapped her hands over them.

Captain Florian snorted. She opened her eyes to see that he had leaned back and still studied her. "Does this spell show what there is to be seen?"

"As if with your own eyes," said Apollonia. "A slightly lower angle, since the eyestones are lower than your eyes."

He snorted again. "You look like an insignificant little lass, then." After a moment, he said, "You looked like that when you first cast it."

"A mouse," said Apollonia, dryly.

He shook his head. "No mouse would—squeak back like you."

Fever and Snow

Pierre lay in the mud, among the bodies, and shivered. It hurt to breathe. He ought to rouse himself, get up—see if any of his comrades lived. Those nearest him lay in pools of blood. No one could bleed that much and live. But others lay farther from him.

He shifted his weight and bit back a moan. His only hope lay in their survival. The warlord still had his army, and he could not stand alone against it, or lie here in the cold and live until they departed and let him rise safely.

He looked about. None of the bodies twitched.

He stared, blankly, and tried to tell himself that it had not been in vain. The flower of the king's chivalry had died, but they had stalled this mysterious warlord who had appeared out of the forest, leading his tribes to pillage and burn. The time might be enough for the king to discover a way to end his slow but endless encroachments. . . but Pierre could not stop shivering.

Footsteps sounded through the ground. The air seemed to grow warmer; it did smell of smoke. Pierre tried to heave to himself up. His chest gave such stabs of pain that he fell to the dirt, gasping for breath and not caring if the warlord killed him where he lay on the earth, as he had sliced the king's knights down in battle.

An honorable death, thought Pierre, dying facing the warlord, not lying in the mud. In spite of the pain, he rolled onto his back. He would face his death openly.

The warlord saw it. After a moment watching Pierre, he strode over. He stood taller than Pierre, and his shoulders were broader—as if that mattered when Pierre was prostrate. His armor, not covered by any tabard, was finest steel—however the tribes had managed to find such stuff—but his helmet was in his hand. His hair and beard were fiery red, about a face the yellow of a candle flame.

The tribesmen are often fair-haired, Pierre told himself.

The beard shifted. Not in the breeze. Pierre felt nauseated. The color was not the only fiery thing about it. It's not fire, he told himself frantically. It's not fire, because smoke does not rise from it, and ashes do not fall. It just shifts like it. . . .

"You fool," said the man, his voice like the rumble of boiling water in a great pot. He crouched beside Pierre. "There is no resisting me. Tell them that—and burn." His mail-clad hand clamped on Pierre's shoulder. Heat surged through the warlord's mail and his own, but did not leave when the warlord rose again. "I burn, I burn, I have no rest—and I have the promise, stronger than steel, that only a child of snow shall destroy me." He strode away.

"My lord," came a scandalized voice. Pierre's gaze flicked over, noticing for the first time the warriors who had accompanied their warlord. None of them wore gear quite as fine as the warlord's, but the man who spoke held his helmet in hand. Of importance, to have that loot.

Not one of the men looked pleased. The man who had spoken spoke again. "You're letting this knave go to plague us again?"

The warlord turned to the man. His beard and hair swirled, like a fire before a draft. The other warriors faded away as the warlord touched that man's shoulder. Smoke rose, and then for a brief minute, open flame and screams of pain.

Pierre, despite his fever, pushed off the ground. His thoughts were quite lucid: he had to escape, in haste. No matter that the warlord had let him go. Only a fool would put any trust in that act.

The warlord's warriors pulled back, with angry and fearful glances at Pierre—and at the warlord. Pierre risked the minutes to ensure that the other knights had not survived. Only after he knew it, did it occur to him that he could have done nothing for any survivor. The warlord had set *him* free.

Tears trickled down in his face, and his hopelessness kept him from even dashing them away.

He staggered down the road, away. What had been a village was now a smoking ruin of ash. Pierre looked away with a shudder. He was not certain that he would have known that the village had stood there if he had not seen it before the battle. Some—a few—villagers and their beasts had escaped, from the number of lumps that lay, unmoving, on the ground.

He staggered on. This was nothing new. The warlord had returned again and again, each time nibbling farther on the kingdom. He scorned to even hear emissaries of peace. It might take decades, but the warlord would swallow the land. Pierre did not know if, feverish as he was, he would be any aid to the king, but he had to escape.

The first warning of the king's camp was the ramshackle tents huddled beside the road, with the dull-eyed and filthy peasants who had escaped the warlord's army. Even the children looked too listless to play. One and all stared at him.

A child of snow, thought Pierre. He staggered on. The king might be able to use that knowledge. But he could not manage to raise his head, even when he heard clamor ahead of him, and voices shouting. Even when a hand closed on his arm.

"Lor' have mercy, you're burning up," exclaimed a knight— whose name Pierre could not quite recall. A babble broke out about him, some speaking of a bed for him to rest.

"I have to speak with the king. The warlord bragged to me." He heard other footsteps. "He told me things. . . ."

"The other knights?" said someone, sharply.

Pierre, unable to answer, closed his eyes.

"I checked," said Pierre dully. "Before I left." The tent all but burst with the king and his generals, the lords of the lands about, the bishops whose dioceses had fallen beneath the warlord's army. His fever burned so fiercely that he could not judge their expressions; his thoughts would not come straight. "They all died."

The king sniffed. "Many a man has assured many a king that his assaults could not be stopped."

Pierre knew how great an honor he enjoyed. The king permitted him to *sit* in his presence. Though he would fall over without the concession, it was an honor. He slumped, putting his face nearer the water pitcher, and the cool water condensing on it.

The king's mouth turned sour. "You have done me a great service, fetching the news in your illness." He sat back. "Return to your native lands, that you may recover to be fit for my service again. As you can not know when that will be, I set no limit on the length of the freedom."

The mountains were cooler than the plains, thought Pierre in longing. He managed to rise to his feet and bow. As he left the tent, it came to him, that with the warlord's slow progress, it might be decades before he reached the mountains. Pierre did not even have the energy to be ashamed of his relief.

The bishop said, behind him, "A child of snow. That is more than anyone else learned of this warlord."

"Indeed, this is no natural illness," murmured Lisette, Pierre's second cousin. Her fingers moved without thought on her knitting, but her gaze did not leave Pierre.

Having told her as much when he first arrived, Pierre sat by the door and watched the mountains. The pine trees shadowing the house did not hold his attention half so much as the clouds billowing up opposite on the purple mountains. The clouds were charcoal gray with the promise of snow—cool, cool, cool snow. With the storm this early, the snow would not last, but he longed for it.

He sighed and leaned back. Lisette and the rest had given him a better welcome than the king had. Unable to bestir himself to do more than look, he doubted that he would impose on their hospitality long.

Lisette lowered her knitting. "The snow woman will come soon. I hope you haven't forgotten her at court. You managed to avoid her all the years you grew up."

Pierre snorted. Once the snow woman's ways had been known, she could catch no one but a foolish stranger. She had haunted the mountains, her ways known, for centuries, for so long that no one could remember where she had come from. The oldest grandfathers could not remember when she had killed someone. "I managed. Had I been as prudent about this warlord, I might have done the same, and been safe—and foresworn."

Lisette's lip curled. "No duty binds you now. Even with your fondness for cool things, if she asks you to hold her baby for her—"

Lisette spoke on, but Pierre did not hear her, feeling as if the snow were already entombing him. The snow woman froze people to death if they accepted the bundle she carried, but those people always had no magical heat themselves, to match her chill.

What choice did he have? He could linger here, imposing on his kin until his death, being of no aid to the king, or he could risk a way to break the spell that destroyed him.

"Did you hear a word I said?" said Lisette.

Pierre smiled on her. "Some. They have been of great aid to me."

Lisette opened her mouth, shut it again, and tilted her head to one side to study him. She could have him restrained, by announcing that he raved. Everyone would believe it of a man so feverish. Pierre smiled at her more broadly. If he perished, he perished; he could not survive this fever forever.

He should go to confession first. The risk was great.

Pierre walked slowly, in the storm and the snowdrifts. The church was the last building in the village, and it vanished into the whiteness behind him. The trees only slowly, and indistinctly, emerged along the way.

Snow pelted down. Against the sky, the flakes looked like a profusion of black dots against the pale gray. Only when he looked at the ground, at the snow that rose up his calves, did he see it as white. But white and snowy as it was, it did not chill him.

You already knew that the warlord's fever is magic, he told himself stoutly. Your toes would feel like chips of ice by now, if the fever did not protect you.

The thought did not hearten him. Pierre looked about. He should stand still. The snow woman would find him more easily.

A gust sent a blast of snowflakes into his face, and Pierre blinked furiously against his watering eyes. The warlord was a true man, even if no one knew his name, even if the tribes whispered fearfully about how he had emerged from the wild forest to seize power. The snow woman having haunted the mountains for centuries, she was something other than human; her magic might overwhelm the warlord's curse and leave him frozen, dead.

Pierre dashed a hand across his eyes, against the tears and the sweat the fever brought to his face. The warlord's men could have butchered him like the rest of the king's knights. He could risk death twice, against the warlord's magic.

He looked up. The snow fell so thickly that he could barely see a stride ahead of himself; he could not have told whether he stood in the forest or fields, or even the mountains or the plains. He stood with his back to the wind, and waited. The snow squall abated; though snowflakes flew to either hand, he could see the trees before him; still, he did not move.

A cry from behind reached him on the wind: "Oh, help me, please help me. . . ." Pierre swallowed at its plaintive note. For a moment, he felt certain that another woman was lost and freezing in the storm, one in dire need, one any knight with any honor would aid. "Oh please, oh help me."

She sounded choked, even on the verge of tears. Pierre turned. The snow blew into his face, sharp crystals brushing against his cheeks, but still he could see.

A woman walked beneath the snow-laden trees. Her mantle was silver gray, and lined with white fur. Beneath the hood, Pierre made out a white face, and a swath of black hair, as black as ice on black rock. He swallowed. In the folds of the mantle, she carried a bundle. It was about the size of an infant, though it was hard to tell, with all the swaddlings. She seemed ready to drop it from sheer exhaustion.

Her face looked as woebegone as any peasant fleeing the warlord, and as she approached, she staggered as if she had been lost in the storm for hours, and weariness and chill overbore her. It had been centuries, Pierre reminded himself, but she looked so miserable. She lifted her face again, and her gaze moved over the snowy scene.

She saw him, and for a moment, all motion ceased in her. Pierre heard his heart hammer, once, twice, thrice.

Her white face was broken by a smile that did not reach her ice-blue eyes, but her voice was sweet and tender. "Oh, sir, oh help me please." When Pierre did not retreat, she drew closer. "Would you hold my baby for me?"

Pierre could not speak; fever or no fever, his tongue had frozen. He held out his arms. She laid the bundle in them. The brush of her fingers was like ice, he could feel it even through the fever, though her face was set in adulation—or what appeared as adulation. "Oh thank you, kind sir, I feared I was ready to perish for the cold and weariness. . . ."

Pierre shifted his burden, and her hands went out. "Careful now, careful," she crooned.

Pierre, having held the infants of friends, jostled the bundle into place, as if supporting a newborn. He stared down at the swathes of cloth. Was there actually a face in there?

The snow woman ceased to smile quite so gratefully. Her forehead creased in perplexity. Pierre shivered at a gust of wind. It worked, he thought. He wondered at it, as if he had never thought of the possibility—but he no longer felt quite so feverish. His face even felt chilled.

The bundle whimpered. Pierre nearly dropped it in surprise: the snow woman actually had a baby? After centuries of wandering the hills? A baby should have grown up—grown old—died of age long ago.

The snow woman looked as shocked as he felt. She stepped toward him. Her voice, though full of menace, was barely audible over the wind. "What are you doing to my baby?"

Without a thought, Pierre pulled the bundle closer. His thoughts formed a muddle, of how much he needed the breaking of his fever, and the dire need to rescue the helpless child from the snow woman—even if it was her baby, she had kept it frozen in infancy for centuries.

The warlord had spoken of a snow child.

The bundle bawled and then screamed, and the snow woman stepped toward him again. Pierre fled. The snow was slick underfoot, and the snowfall heavy enough to make his path hard to trace, but he had to escape.

He glanced back. The snow woman billowed up to loom like a storm cloud. "WHAT ARE YOU DOING WITH MY BABY?"

Pierre ran. Winds buffeted his back. From the way the snow beat at him, the snowfall contained splinters of hail. The bundle yelped and wailed, but he had no time to even consider. The snow woman had risen up so high than her shadow fell over him, greater than a mountain's. He no longer sweated, even running at full speed. His toes and fingers felt like ice.

The church, he thought. The church stood ahead.

God have mercy, let him find the church, let the shelter protect him from this monster.

His foot slid out from under him across a patch of ice. The baby shrieked as he lurched, and steadied himself, and ran on through the snow. If he missed the village, he would perish, and the child would perish, when he fled over some cliff...

As a dark shadow in the white air, the church loomed out of the snow, more sudden than the snow woman's appearance among the pines. His breath coming hoarsely enough to mask the baby's protests, Pierre staggered around the building to the door. His free hand, chilled to numbness, managed, with some difficulty, to wrap fingers about the door handle, and tug at the door. It slid a fraction and caught, revealing no more than a dark crack. Not daring to put the baby down where the snow woman could reach, he set his mouth and yanked harder on the door. It creaked open.

Pierre staggered within. The candlelight faintly lit the stonework. Pierre saw a shadow move toward him, but had no time to look. He laid the bundle on the flagstones and turned to close the door. It caught on the snow. His mouth set, Pierre put two hands to it, and it moved, though slowly.

"Why, what are you doing about here, on this night?" said Father Jean, baffled.

Pierre gritted his teeth. "Trying to shut the door."

"What could be so urgent?" The priest stiffened. "You are not trying to trap some poor creature out there?"

"Father, if you wish to preach to the snow woman, do so! If not, help me!"

Muttering about insolence, Father Jean nonetheless helped him shut it against the wind and snow.

The bundle screamed again.

"There's a poor creature for you," said Pierre with satisfaction. His sojourn here was not a waste but a service to the king. Snow child—the warlord had not reckoned that such predictions always foretold a possibility. In spite of his chilled face, Pierre smiled as the priest went to inspect. The warlord had boasted too much: now the prophesied child would know of it. "He will grow up to be a great knight and defeat the warlord—"

Father Jean rose, having pulled back the blankets. A child lay in his arm—dark-haired, tiny, not more than a month old, and female. "Will she?"

Pierre blinked—but the prediction was not his. Perhaps some other means of destroying the warlord would reveal itself in time. "Yes, she will."

"Why?" said the priest. "An innocent child?" He scowled. "Where did you get her?"

"From the snow woman." Father Jean's scowl deepened. a Pierre explained. Father Jean looked as if he realized he was holding a goblin. He darted down the aisle.

Pierre raced after, but before he could reach him, the priest dunked the baby in the holy water fount. She screamed. When Pierre reached him, Father Jean had wrapped her up in a blanket again and was soothing her. She looked as she had before, and no more than indignant at being dunked.

"She must be baptized," said the priest. "That will protect her from the snow woman."

It could only help, thought Pierre. He looked at the wooden statues about the church. "I will be her godfather, and she shall be named—Marie-Neige, that she may be under the protection of Our Lady of the Snows."

"A good name," said Lisette, bending over the cradle to tease Marie-Neige's cheek. The snow's melting had made the paths as passable as they had been before the storm. The other village woman walked by her house, whispering among themselves, but they did not press in as they would at a birth, or if an orphan babe had arrived at a kinswoman's house.

A babe—Pierre laughed at himself. Likely, Marie-Neige was older than every grandfather in the village.

"You will have an interesting time looking after her."

Pierre felt his face contort.

Lisette laughed. "I saw the king's reward for your fidelity—you could not afford to have Marie-Neige fostered."

"Just because these mountains are in the heart of the realm—you would not like if the warlord reached here," said Pierre, defensively. "The king has to deal with the warlord."

"And you, with Marie-Neige," said Lisette. "Fortunately, many a poor widower has managed to raise a baby."

"With the aid," said Pierre firmly, "of his female relations and neighbors."

Marie-Neige yowled.

Lisette bent over her again. "Yes, my little darling—he has me there. I must concede the point, but our best help will be showing him how to do it."

As the months passed—into spring, summer, and fall—Marie-Neige flourished, and Pierre grew accustomed to taking care of the fierce little baby, even when she threw her dinner on floor. In the summer heat, she crawled about as if it were the most natural thing in the world, and the town slowly came to view her as a child.

The winter came, bringing its cohort of snowstorms, and rumors started: the snow woman haunted the town; the snow woman no longer asked wanderers to hold her baby but, outraged, demanded it of them; the snow woman chased after longer and harder than she ever had when someone refused to hold her baby, and the air about grew colder. Pierre heard the tales, muttered to him at the tavern or outside the church.

Then a story came, of frostbite and lost toes. Though the man had foolishly ventured out where he could have frozen on his own, the murmurs were behind Pierre's back. In the village, he drew sidelong glances, and more when he brought Marie-Neige. Father Jean preached several stern sermons on charity and hospitality, and nothing more happened of it than the glances, but those glances did not stop.

Years inched by. Though the snow woman grew not a whit less persistent, care meant no one else lost fingers or toes, and the murmurs died down. Marie-Neige sprouted into childhood and, in her taciturnity, shortened her name to Neige. In the wintertime, Pierre discovered that Neige did not grow quite as cold as other children did; she would shiver without her coat and her blankets, but the weather grew much colder before she needed them. That, he never mentioned to another, even Lisette or Father Jean.

Word filtered up from the plains, that the warlord was conquering the land, however slowly, and the king was unable to stop him, that no one had discovered the secrets of why he burned so fierily. Pierre took new strength from the rumors, especially when Neige hid under the table to sulk.

One fall day when she was six, Neige went nutting in the forest, with the other girls. A storm gathered in the west, great clouds piling up. Her apron full of nuts, Neige stopped to watch. The sunlight still shone on the forest, but it did not warm the air as it had in the summer.

"That'll snow," said one of the older girls. "We had best get home."

"Or it will hit us," said the littlest girl. She shivered melodramatically. "And the snow woman will come and try to get us to hold her baby—"

Sidelong glances looked at Neige. She glared back. The girls turned their attention back to their nuts. Neige poured her nuts into her basket and snatched it up to hurry with the rest of them.

The storm came faster than it had seemed to move. Within moments, the girls were engulfed in the clouds' shadows, and within minutes, wind yanked at their skirts and their hair, carrying stinging snowflakes with it.

"I see her!" one girl wailed. "The snow woman!" Neige, dubious, looked about, but in the falling snow, a woman's shape, larger than any woman had any right to be, loomed in the whiteness.

Then someone's foot interposed between Neige's ankles. Neige went sprawling, nuts cascading from her basket. Ghislaine cast a triumphant glance over her shoulder and disappeared with the other girls into the snow.

Neige pushed off the snowy ground and wondered, for a bewildered moment, about the nuts. Sitting up on the snow and fallen leaves, she grabbed the basket handle and pulled it into her lap. The remaining nuts rattled.

"WHAT HAVE YOU DONE WITH MY BABY?"

A shadow loomed over her, and an enraged face looked down. "WHERE IS MY BABY? WHAT HAVE YOU DONE WITH MY BABY?"

Neige gawked, sprang to her feet, and ran, the nuts rattling with every step.

"You did *what*?"

In the shelter of the common barn, with the children swarming about, Ghislaine's mother looked torn between slapping her daughter silly and dreading Pierre. Though the woman had been among the foremost giver of sidelong glances, Pierre could not rouse up anger against the little girl—not when he dreaded what would happen to Neige. Would the snow woman be able to turn her back into a baby? Would she be so enraged that Neige had grown that she would kill her? Neige did not feel the cold as other children did, but she felt it; she could not endure the snow woman's attack.

All about the barn, no matter how often they had muttered about Neige, women drew their daughters back from Ghislaine and her mother.

Footsteps echoed on the road. Neige came pelting down it, through the snow, visible through the open door. Her clothing was mussed, but Pierre saw no sign of injury. Her gaze went over the crowd and settled on Pierre; she followed it, her arms outstretched. Pierre bent to receive her, and she clasped her arms about his neck, and her legs about his waist. The nuts in her basket rattled.

"Papa," she said in satisfaction, her head against his shoulder.

Pierre put her back a little, so he could see his goddaughter's face. "Are you all right?"

Neige nodded.

"We were worried, about the snow woman." Pierre pushed back her black hair from Neige's face.

Neige nodded again. "Saw her. 'What have you done with my baby?'" She pointed at herself and grinned. "To *me*."

The gasps resounded at that. A voice came from the back of the barn. "Then our course is clear." Father Jean drew all attention to himself with that remark. "All babies must be baptized as soon as may be—that aided our Marie-Neige—and kept watch over, lest the snow woman take one as her own."

"Should have left her the one she had," someone muttered— but Pierre could not pick out who, and Neige did not seem to hear. He ignored it.

Neige wriggled to be put down.

"What is it, Neige?" said Pierre.

Neige pointed at Ghislaine. "Nuts," she said, holding up her basket. "She owes me."

Ghislaine yielded up nuts to replace those she had spilled, and the years went by. The snow woman raged and haunted the villages in the winter, but the grumbles slowly faded as she seemed, like snowstorms, to be just one peril of the mountains.

When the news came, in the winter that Neige was twelve, that the king had had to retreat into the mountains, Pierre found that more distressing than the snow woman's presence. The rumor reached him at his home, and he ventured into the village to hear. The messenger stood by the alewife's door, drinking the mulled ale and proclaiming his news again. "King's by the first pass already—or was when I left him. He'll be at the mountain castle by now."

The man drained his ale. "I'll have to venture on tomorrow. He sent me to bear news across the mountains."

Not to me, of course, thought Pierre. He dismissed me with no time to return and knows no reason why he needs my presence. His gaze went past the messenger, to the girls throwing snowballs. Neige's cheeks were as red as apples.

"Where's this warlord?" said a woman in the crowd.

"The river by now," said the messenger. "He hadn't turned his attention to the mountains before."

Pierre shifted his weight. Perhaps the king's forces could not stop the warlord's, but they could hamper it. The battle he had fought in had hindered the warlord. And now they had a reason to lengthen the time: until Neige grew up.

Pierre swallowed. Better than he could, the king could hide Neige where the warlord would not find her, until she discovered the way she would destroy the warlord. It was Pierre's duty both to protect his goddaughter for as long as possible, and to show the king that there was a way to protect the kingdom.

He let out a long breath. When he had rescued Neige, that had been part of his purpose. When it came to the deed, the quiet life here seemed more pleasant. That did not mean that his duty was unclear.

In the blue mid-afternoon, Neige rode her pony in stolid silence, even when the melting snow fell in white lumps from the tree boughs on her head. Stolid silence even for her.

Pierre watched the road. It was a narrow track at best. Between the winter's few travelers and the snowfall, only a careful eye could pick it out. A misstep could send them wandering in the forest for weeks.

Neige would not object to that, even if the snow woman plagued them again; she had haunted them three evenings already, whenever it snowed.

Pierre shook his head. Raising a child had meant many occasions of denying Neige her desire. This was just another, and he had his duty to his goddaughter. It was not only the realm's safety that was at risk.

"What's that?" said Neige.

Her first words that day had Pierre blinking. Neige did not stir, staring down into the valley, at an encampment—clearly an armed one.

"An army," said Pierre.

Neige shook her head. "Not that. *That.*" She pointed, at one figure in the camp: a reddish figure, moving among the tents, large among the soldiers. Even against the snow's whiteness, he seemed to glow.

Pierre's breath hissed between his teeth. Even as injured as he had been, even lying in the mud, he would have seen if the warlord had glowed like that. Years would not have erased that memory. Perhaps the warlord had grown more fiery. Watching how he paced and paced among the tents, Pierre remembered his claim of restlessness.

"That," said Pierre, solemnly, "is the evil warlord. No one knows where he comes from, but he is conquering the land, killing the peasants and ruining the crops. He killed my fellow knights and cursed me with a fever, to kill me slowly, before I rescued you from the snow woman."

Neige said, "The fever was how you rescued me."

"So it was," said Pierre, and wondered how to encourage this unaccustomed burst of loquacity, but his imagination failed him. They rode on in silence.

Another camp appeared in the next valley, and Neige turned her gaze on her godfather. A gust of wind blew on the blue and silver banner, and Pierre had a glimpse of the swan to confirm.

"That's the king's."

Neige did not seem moved by the information. Pierre glanced at the sky. It was already orange and pink with encroaching evening, and the color lay on new clouds, billowing up in the west. That the camp was clear to them did not mean that the road led straight to it; valleys and forests lay between, and Pierre thought he remembered a river. With this snow melt, he could not be sure that the ice would bear his and Neige's weight.

He groaned. When Neige lifted her eyebrows, he kicked his horse's sides and rode down the road again. There was nothing she, or he, could do about this.

The sky turned gray with cloud, and the clouds grew hazy about the edges, as if releasing their burdens. Pierre stiffened. When the first snowflakes came down, from a sky gray more with evening than with storm, he resolved to go on, into the night. The snow woman could arrive in a storm like this.

A voice echoed against the hills: "What have you done with my baby?"

They both looked over. No sign of the snow woman or the hapless traveler could be seen; Pierre could only be glad the snow woman had found another and would not prey on them yet, and shame at his own relief. "Lord have mercy on her victim."

They rode on, and another voice rose ahead: a man's voice, echoing, and bellowing in rage even so. "I will destroy you, and all your men, and all your subjects."

"The warlord?" said Neige.

Pierre nodded. They rode on and over a slope and saw the warlord. Under the cloudy sky, in the snow, it was clear that he *did* glow. Pierre shuddered in memory. He fancied he could see the snow melting in the air about the warlord.

The warlord looked up the path and directly at them. Pierre, startled, pulled up his horse before he thought.

"Come to join this regal fool?" shouted the warlord. "I will destroy you!"

Pierre spoke in a low voice and hoped that the warlord's magic did not extend to his hearing. "We will be safer among the king's forces. Come, let us go."

Neige shook her head. "His fever," she said. "The snow woman's cold. They cancelled out." Her face was pale in the gloom, almost as pale as the snow woman's.

Pierre eyed her warily, but lying to Neige was always foolish. He nodded.

Neige grunted in satisfaction, turned her horse's head, and kicked its sides. The horse trundled off, back along the road. Pierre yanked on his horse's reins. "Neige, I forbid you—"

Neige kicked her horse's sides again. It leapt off faster than a horse had any right to run after being ridden all day. Casting maledictions on her head, frantic with worry, Pierre turned his own horse to follow her. Though he tried for speed, Neige kept ahead of him, even when she left the road for the drifts. Then, his heart seemed to stop for a long minute, before it hammered the harder. He could not have told the direction for certain, but he knew that she headed toward the snow woman.

As if hunting down the snow woman. . . .

Pierre pulled up his horse. Ahead of him, Neige dismounted and ran from her horse. It raised its head and whinnied. Pierre set his horse through the snows again to grab the reins of Neige's steed. He drew in a deep breath, chilling his lungs. What did Neige think she was about?

"WHAT DID YOU DO TO MY BABY?"

Pierre flinched. Neige had vanished into the snow and woods as he pondered. He could barely make out her tracks. Soon the evening would turn to a stormy night, and all would be invisible. Lord have mercy on us all, he prayed.

"What a fool you are," said Neige, as coldly as the air.

"HOW DARE YOU?"

Pierre, envisioning the snow woman looming over Neige, closed his eyes. He could feel the chill where he stood. Neige could lose fingers or toes in this insanity—or life itself.

"Call you a fool?" Neige's voice was contemptuous. "You are a fool."

The snow woman billowed up. "WHERE IS MY BABY?"

"*I* can't tell you where your baby is," said Neige, sullenly, but showing no signs of falling silent.

People had suffered frostbite fleeing her. Standing and telling her that she had no hope—how much cold could the snow woman inflict? Pierre staggered forward.

"WHERE IS MY BABY?"

"I heard a man *threaten* your baby, not an hour past," said Neige. "You don't care much about her, letting him be."

Pierre stopped. His heart hammered. After a moment, he thought—she had, after all.

"YOU LIE, YOU LIE!"

Pierre could hear the shrug in Neige's voice. "All right, I lie. Nothing to me whether you care about your baby."

"You lie! There is no such man."

Pierre let out his breath in a gust. Only indecision could have the snow woman lowering her voice thus, and now he knew no more than the snow woman what to do. Neige was doing something, and if she was not so clever as she thought she was, she had her wits about her.

He knew who the man was—but the warlord had spoken of a *child* of snow.

"If you cared about your baby, you would listen—but you don't. You just want to bother me."

"You lie, you little wretch."

"I can *show* you," said Neige.

Pierre yanked on the reins of Neige's horse. She would have to backtrack. He did not think it wise to be found on that track—for either him or the horses. He did not dare risk disturbing her fascination with Neige's words, and Neige would need the horse, afterward.

God willing, she would need her horse, after.

Neige plugged through the drifts. Her gaze went past Pierre as if she did not see him. Her walk was unsteady, but the snow woman watched with such focus that Pierre did not dare approach.

Ever-living God, Pierre prayed, let Neige need the horse afterwards.

"There he is," caroled Neige. She and the snow woman stood on the hill, in the tree's shadow. Neige pointed into the valley, to where the warlord glowed in the twilight. Neige added, her voice deeper, "The one who threatened your baby. I heard him."

The snow woman did not stir. Neige pulled to one side, out of the snow woman's path, and the snow woman's gaze remained intent. Neige crept away.

She was out of danger, for a moment. Pierre dismounted. Neige bolted across the snow to throw her arms about him. She felt icy, and trembled like a life in a high wind. He held her close, putting his mantle about, before Neige turned to watch the snow woman. Cold or no cold, Pierre only ensured that the mantle still covered her before he also watched.

The warlord paused in his endless pacing, and his face contorted with fury. Even at this distance, Pierre could see the snow melting about him, and the warlord's men drew back. "If you have come to join them, you will die with them!"

The warlord shook his fist at the snow woman. His glow and the campfires were the bare light the scene had.

Neige pressed close to Pierre, shivering. "Father, can't he *see*?"

Pierre followed her gaze. The looming snow woman did not look much like an ordinary mortal, and the warlord seemed oblivious. "Perhaps he thinks his magic is stronger."

Despite the blazing warlord, the air grew colder. Pierre could feel it where he stood, and snow formed in the air about the snow woman, like a veiling cloud. "WHAT HAVE YOU DONE WITH MY BABY?"

The warlord flinched, for the first time looking hesitant. Then he seemed to grow, like fire that first shrank as wood was added, and then leapt as the wood took blaze. "I have slaughtered mere babes by the score! Who are you to call me to account for them? I WILL SHOW YOU TO PESTER ME FOR SUCH INSIGNIFICANCE!"

The snow woman swept down the hillside, snow and cold trailing behind her. The warlord climbed it to meet her, sparks flying from him, water streaming from his steps. The snow in the air before her reached him and melted into fog. The snow woman charged on, and the snowy air engulfed them. Fog and snow both surrounded them. Steam billowed, and the sound like fire fizzling to nothing in water. Water flooded from the fog, soaking the snow outside, and washing it away. Steam puffed out, and Pierre felt a blast like heat.

"I," said Neige softly. Her arms tightened about his neck. "I didn't think it'd be *that* bad."

Pierre glanced about. The king's men still gawked, but the warlord's slowly withdrew, abandoning their tents, grabbing only what they could grab in haste. Pierre let out his breath. Neige did not look away from the fight.

Sparks and ice pellets flew from the cloud, and the cloud spread. Pierre, rather than argue, swept her up and over one shoulder to walk away, leading the horses. Neige did not struggle, but Pierre could feel her craning her neck to watch.

The light snowfall had dusted where the fight had occurred, but the snow of earlier had been melted down to the dirt: the earth was still visible. Wet earth.

"I do not get it," said Pierre.

Neige tilted her head to one side.

"The warlord said that only a child of snow could destroy him. The woman was not a child."

"But *I* led them together," said Neige.

"You didn't need to be a child of snow for that," said Pierre. "Anyone could talk like that."

Neige looked indignant. "Anyone *didn't. I* did." She pirouetted, and Pierre watched her. She scowled and kicked him in the ankle. "Tell me how clever I was to have thought of it."

It occurred to Pierre that possibly no one else could have endured the cold to argue with the snow woman, but Neige shouldn't have kicked him if she wanted to hear that. He threw his arms about her shoulders, lifted her up, and twirled her around. "You are," he whispered in her ear, "so incredibly silly to abuse your poor loving godfather."

Neige giggled.

"Sir Pierre!" The king strode across the snow.

Pierre eased Neige back to the ground. Neige slacked her grip but did not release his hand.

The king looked at Neige and did not, quite, sniff. "I salute your loyalty, in coming to my aid." He gestured at the gap. "Though it is not needed, it is valued."

It was not needed indeed, thought Pierre. I told you about the child of snow. He opened his mouth.

"Home," whispered Neige.

He remembered all the years of her growing up. If he returned to the king's service, he might see Neige once a year. If that—the king might declare that Neige was his fosterling and not his daughter. He closed his mouth and bowed.

The king looked at the gap in the snow again. "Abide the night with us, Sir Pierre. Return to your home in the morning."

Pierre bowed again. The king and his knights returned to the camp. Pierre stood over the fight scene a while longer. No one knew where the snow woman had come from, because she had haunted the hills for so long. Or perhaps no one had ever learned, any more than they had discovered it for the warlord.

"I wonder," said Neige, "if she's found out what happened to her baby."

After a minute, Pierre said, "I wonder if he's no longer restless." He took Neige's hand and walked down with her into the king's camp. "Come and warm yourself at the fire." Neige hummed under her breath, and Pierre thought, with pleasure, that the snow woman would never realize that her baby had grown up. Neige would remain with him forever. He stopped to embrace her. Neige, after a moment of surprise, threw her arms about his neck.

Also by Mary Catelli

Magic of the Lost God
Never Comment On A Likeness
One Name
The Drunken Mermaids
The Turtle in the Sea of Sand
Were I You
Where There Is Smoke